RENDEZVOUS AT BITTER WELLS

Under a blazing desert sun, Wes Martin lay trapped between hostile Chiricahuas and an Army column, waiting to die. With him was a man he had met just that morning, who was already almost buzzard bait, and who was offering Wes a third of a map that held part of a secret to a fortune—if Wes managed to survive.

That miracle did occur. But Wes still had the task of making rendezvous in Bitter Wells with the two men who had the rest of the map before his piece could be of any use.

But one of the two men was killed before Wes could meet with him—and the third man was nowhere in sight . . .

RENDEZVOUS AT BITTER WELLS

Jim Kane

GUNSMOKE

This hardback edition 2002
by Chivers Press
by arrangement with
Golden West Literary Agency

ISBN 0 7540 8159 1

British Library Cataloguing in Publication Data available.

Printed and bound in Great Britain by
BOOKCRAFT, Midsomer Norton, Somerset

RENDEZVOUS AT BITTER WELLS

— I —

— THE LONG SHOT —

WES MARTIN watched the big red orb of the splinter itself on the craggy hills west of the Colorado and unemotionally contemplated which way he would die.

South of the river, where the bald and weathered buttes bared grim edges to the paling sky, the smoke of a council fire plumed up over the camp of the Chiricahuas, seeming to hold within its tenuous image the reflections of a savage anger and remembrance of broken treaties.

Far to the eastward, a long day's march already behind them, moved Major Kennedy's column, heading for a junction at Salt Lick. Major Kennedy had his orders. Make contact with Bearpaw and his angry warriors and push them back onto the reservation. . . .

Somewhere between the two main bodies Wes

9

Martin was trapped. He squatted on his heels in the dubious shelter of a rock nest. His right forearm rested across his thighs a Colt nestled in his palm. . . . He watchd the long shadows come stealing like wary coyotes across the parched and empty land and knew they came too late to do him any good.

He had been there all day at the mercy of the blazing desert sun—crouched and waiting—while his long, leather-tough body, already dehydrated by years in that furnace heat, began to dry up and die.

He sat in the rocks with the tantalizing vision of a cool, green-bordered water hole less than two hundred yards away. Sat there and waited, knowing that this time they had him, and that before the next sun rose some Chiricahua buck would be boasting that he had the scalp of Wes Martin, crack scout for the 12th U.S. Cavalry. Wes faced the inescapable fact squarely, and the wrinkles deepened around his blue eyes. He was too experienced a hand in that parched and eroded land, and he knew the Chiricahuas. They would sit on that water hole and wait patiently— wait until thirst and the desert sun drove him out.

10

Behind him a man coughed, his spasm choked by a sudden inrush of blood. Wes turned and eyed the dying man with dispassionate eyes. A Chiricahua arrow had been driven deep between his shoulder blades . . . he had lingered on longer than West had expected.

The man said, "Hey, mister. . . ." His voice was thin, urgent. Wes hesitated a moment, then eased back to him.

"Water," the man said. "I'm burnin' up. . . ."

Wes said: "Sorry. . . ." He made a gesture toward the waterhole. "They've got it all over there. . . ."

The man tried to push himself up higher against the rock; he tried to see. He was a broad, stocky man, perhaps thirty, thirty-five . . . it was hard to tell. The lines in his stubbled face might be pain lines. He looked like a saddle bum, a man gone sloppy with the years, shiftless, living from day to day. . . .

"Darn savages." He sagged down, fighting the pain in his chest, the slow draining away of his strength. He didn't want to die, and bitterly his will held death at bay. Wes' eyes reflected some admiration for the man.

11

"Got to get away," the man muttered. "Got to . . ." He lapsed into silence and closed his eyes, and Wes turned quickly, sensing movement in the clearing below.

A buzzard drifted down out of the paling sky to join the others quarreling over the carcass of his roan. Wes' glance reached out to the scene, a scant seventy-five yards from where he crouched.

His canteen lay in plain view on the hot sand, still held by its leather thong to his saddle. But a Chiricahua arrow had been driven through it, spilling its contents through the ragged hole into the thirsty sand.

Conserving their ammunition, he thought wryly, and speculated with ironic humor on the reaction of those painted warriors when they found out he had only three bullets left; that the rest of the shiny brass catridges in his belt loops fitted only the Winchester that still lay snugged in the saddle scabbard pinned under his horse.

That rifle meant the difference between life and death to Wes Martin. With it he had a chance of survival. Without it—

12

The dying man stirred and plucked at Wes' arm with fingers that lacked strength.

"What day is it?"

Wes turned and eyed the man. "Tuesday," he replied. He wondered why it seemed to matter to this man.

"May fifth?"

Wes nodded. May fifth—his last day on earth. How would it look on his tombstone? Wesley J. Martin, Born 1847—

The dying man sighed deeply. "Had an appointment on the seventeenth." A lifetime of hope faded slowly. "Place called Bitter Wells."

Wes shrugged. He had an appointment, too . . . with Major Kennedy at Salt Lick Junction.

"Looks like we won't be keeping any appointments," he said quietly.

A Chiricahua showed up on the edge of the water hole, his rifle held across his waist. He stood in plain view, lean and arrogant, daring the man in the rocks, and Wes had to choke back the savage impulse to waste a shot at him.

Behind him the dying man said: "They've got us, haven't they?"

Wes didn't saying anything. He tried to swal-

13

low, but his mouth was too dry. He felt his gun arm begin to tremble slightly from the strain, and he eased the heavy weapon down, resting it on his knee again.

"Guess—no use fighting it—" the man behind him said. He hunched himself up slightly and tried to peer over Wes' shoulder toward the far, ragged hills.

"Darn shame." His voice was low, bitter. "One hundred and fifty thousand dollars waiting. . . ."

His voice faded, and he closed his eyes, and Wes ignored him. The sun was down now, but there was no apparent lessening of the heat. It was quiet in the rocks, but the buzzards quarreling over the carcass of his horse suddenly sickened him, and in a savage gust of anger he fired into them, wasting one precious shot before control came back to him.

The ungainly scavengers lifted into the air as the explosion rocked the stillness, leaving one of their companions writhing on the sand. By the waterhole, the Chiricahua warriors turned and faded from sight among the brush. . . .

Wes rocked back on his heels and eyed the two cartridges left in his chamber. Might as well

14

make a run for it now—

The man behind him said: "Mister . . ." and Wes turned, slightly surprised. He had thought the man was dead.

"Owe you something for trying to help. . . ."

He was fumbling inside his coat pocket. His hand came out, gripping a small chamois poke that appeared empty. He held it out to Wes.

"Take it." His hand dropped weakly by his side, and he took a deep breath. "Piece of paper inside . . . worth fifty thousand dollars."

Wes humored him. "Thanks," he said dryly. "But I won't have a chance to spend it."

He started to ease away, but the man's fingers gripped him, holding him.

"You still got a chance." He held up the poke, and Wes took it, frowning.

"Name's Joe Seltzer," the man said. "Had a rendezvous . . . small desert town in Arizona . . . had to be there on the seventeenth." He paused, and a fleck of blood appeared at a corner of his mouth. He tried to wipe it away but didn't have the strength.

"Waited five years," he said finally. His voice was bitter. "Broke most of the time . . . drifting

15

. . . panhandling meals." His chuckle was a small dry sound in his throat. "Didn't care . . . knew about the money, see . . . knew about the money, see . . . knew I'd be rich."

Wes frowned. He picked up the poke. He could feel the hard outlines of two coins inside, the rustle of a slip of paper.

"Three of us left," Joe went on. "Me, Oley Jones and Cory Bates. Each man has a map . . . need all three to find the money . . . buried out there."

He closed his eyes, and his hand well away from Wes' arm.

"Yours," he whispered. "My share . . . it's yours . . . if you . . . you. . . ."

His voice faded, and the breath went out of him in a soft sigh. And then, sharply, as if voicing a grim epitaph, three bullets spaced split-seconds apart gouged and whined off the rocks a few feet above them.

Wes whirled, his gun coming up, hammer back. He held himself in time and cursed softly, eyeing the warrior who had fired the shots.

They were baiting them, trying to drive him out. . . . He wondered how long it would take

16

before they decided to come in after him.

He settled back and waited. It had been a long day . . . he could wait a little longer.

He glanced at the dead man propped against the rocks behind him—a man he had never seen until that morning. . . .

Wes shifted his weight and glanced off toward the east, where the sky was already darkening. He had been riding far ahead of Major Kennedy's column and had found the main camp of the Chiricahuas before dawn. An hour's patient vigil had been enough to ascertain the strength of Bearpaw's party, the number of bootlegged rifles and the fact that the war party was awaiting reinforcements before moving out. This done, he had withdrawn without detection and was riding for Salt Lick Junction when he had run into Joe Seltzer.

Joe had an arrow in his back and was running from a Chiricahua scouting party. Wes had the choice of leaving the man to die or trying to help. He had made his choice without hesitation, and they had almost reached the safety of the rocks when a bullet had killed Wes' horse. He had managed to get into the rocks with Seltzer, but it was

17

a temporary shelter, and time was running out fast.

Wes considered the odds. It was more than two hundred yards to the water hole. When the time came, when his thirst became unbearable, he'd have to make his play. A break for his rifle—or a charge for the water hole and a quick death.

He shifted again, easing cramped leg muscles. Dissatisfaciton stirred in him. He was a lean, sun-browned man, pushing thirty; he had been on his own since he had turned fourteen. And he had nothing to show for it. The only thing he owned was out there, between him and that water hole— a dead horse, a saddle, a rifle, and a few personal items wrapped up in his slicker roll.

It was a devil of a way to die.

He came alert, sneering at his momentary lapse into self-pity. He stared off coldly as a warrior came up to the water hole to stand beside the one who had fired the rifle shots. He was holding a canteen in his hand as he stared toward the rocks where Wes waited. He lifted the canteen to his lips and drank slowly. Water dribbled down his chin and across his bare chest. The fading light caught the trickles and turned them to silver

18

rivulets, and Wes slowly laid his Colt muzzle across the rock in front of him and targeted the Apache. But he did not fire.

That's what they want, he thought grimly.

There were five of them at the water hole, armed with rifles and bows. There had been six, but one of them had ridden away at midday, heading for the main camp.

There was a red banner against the western horizon now where the sun had gone down. In a few more minutes it would be dark.

Wes Martin made his decision then. He would make a break for the rifle. *The sooner the better,* he thought bleakly, *while he still had a clear head.* He didn't expect to make it, but he couldn't sit and die there among the rocks. Three of the Chiricahuas were now silhouetted against the pale green sky, and one of them waved a hand toward the east.

"Blast you," Wes muttered. "If I had that Winchester, I'd show you a thing or two. I'd make you think you had run into the whole 12th Cavalry."

A thought hit him then, cutting sharply across his confined anger. If he could reach them with

19

one lucky shot, the surprise it would create might give him a chance to reach his rifle.

Two cartridges loaded with black powder. There was one way to get more distance. *Add more powder!*

He went to work then, using his teeth to extract the lead from the cartridge cases. Very carefully he added powder from one of the shell cases to the other. He replaced the lead slug, pushing it carefully into place. The added powder thrust the lead nose farther outward, but the bullet slipped easily into firing position, and Wes Martin smiled grimly. He was banking everything on this one shot.

The Chiricahuas were still standing in front of the water hole, their lean bodies silhouetted against the paling sky. Wes eased the Colt barrel forward, targeted the warrior who had taken the long drink and pulled the trigger.

The Chiricahua spun around and fell as the report broke the evening stillness. The buzzards wheeling slowly overhead scattered; the remaining two warriors at the water hole broke ground and ran. Wes was out of the rocks and running as they turned.

20

He reached the roan without receiving a return shot in his direction. Kneeling by the animal, he tore at his Winchester, pulling it free. A cold and deadly rage pulsed through him, making him light-headed with its offer of hope. He turned and sought one of the Chiricahuas in his sights, and the sharp bite of the repeater kicked the man backward and out of sight.

The others had vanished. Wes went running toward the water hole, holding his cocked rifle across his body. There was a small, grassy gouge in the dry earth past the water hole where the overflow from the springs lost itself. The Chiricahuas had picketed their ponies there.

Wes Martin caught the remaining three bucks as they were mounting. He picked two off before they got started. The last one ducked out of sight along his wiry mustang's neck and made the top of the embankment before Martin got around to him.

The scout took his time, leading the running animal in his sights. He placed his shot so that it tore through the animal's neck just below the brushy mane, and a quick vision of that slug smashing into the Chiricahua on the other side

21

gave him a grim and sudden satisfaction.

The pony went down in a twisting header, tossing his rider free. The Chiricahua didn't move.

Wes walked slowly to the water hole. He stopped and drank thirstily but sparingly, and after a while his jaws loosened and saliva started again in his mouth. He reached into his pockets for the makings . . . and found Joe Seltzer's chamois pouch instead.

He turned and looked back to the rocks where the man's body lay huddled.

"Rendezvous at Bitter Wells," he muttered softly. Maybe there was something to the man's story; maybe this was the break he had been looking for all his life.

He walked back toward the rocks for Joe's body.

Ten minutes later, mounted on a wiry Chiricahua pony and leading another with Joe's body slung over it, he headed for Salt Lick Junction. . . .

– II –

– CORY BATES –

FIVE YEARS had not changed Bitter Wells, Cory thought. But they had changed him. He felt their dreary passage weigh on him as he stepped down from the spring wagon and turned to pay the thin-lipped man who had brought him to the badlands town from Caldwell Junction.

"Ten dollars," the man said, and took the bill Cory handed him without expression. He was a shrewd old man who made occasional deliveries there from Caldwell Junction, and he was going back in the morning. He told Cory so.

"Will you be going back with me?" he asked Cory. Cory shook his head, and the old man looked at him for a bit, wondering what business

23

Cory could have in that squalid desert town. Then he turned and drove away.

Cory stood in the dust of the wide street, his battered suitcase at his feet. The high riding sun beat down on him, a tall, round-shouldered man, only vaguely conscious of the curious stares of the loafers on the sagging veranda of the town's hotel. Five years had faded the sign's black paint so that it was barely readable. Sun and weather had cracked the wide pine board on which the sign was painted, and it was indicative of the town's civic spirit that no attempt had been made to replace it.

A hundred yards up or down the dusty road from the hotel, and a man was out of Bitter Wells. The heat lay in shimmering waves over the sage flats surrounding the town.

He was facing northwest, and his gaze sought out the dark blue bulk of a butte in the badlands. Behind that wind-shaped mass the badlands ran into the high desert country of New Mexico—he remembered that scorched, eroded land with a clarity undimmed by the years.

Rocky Callahan had died there, and the limping blond kid from Sioux Falls—Voss Grant.

They were buried there, along with one hundred and fifty thousand dollars in crisp new bills—or bills that had been new five years ago.

Of the five men who had held up the crack express train that night, there were only three left: Oley Jones, Joe Seltzer and himself, Cory Bates.

Three men who had agreed to meet here in Bitter Wells, five years later.

The lines in Corey's face were deep-drawn, and impatience had left its mark on him. He was not yet thirty, but he looked older. For four of the past five years he had lived a lie—he had served as an indifferent deputy sheriff of Tolliver County.

The remembrance made him feel uneasy now. He had hidden behind that deputy's badge, waiting for this moment—for this rendezvous at Bitter Wells. Five long years spent living out a lie—not really living at all. Waiting for time to go by so he could come back here to claim his share of that buried money.

Had it been worth it?

As Cory stood by the rickety two-story frame hotel, he wasn't sure.

25

He was conscious now of the watchers on the veranda, of the creaking cane-bottom rocker in which a paunchy, thick-shouldered Mexican sprawled. Cory let his glance run over these men, not finding the faces he sought. He wondered if Oley and Joe were already there.

They had separated at this very spot in front of the hotel, each man riding his own particular trail. He had not seen any of them since.

"We'll meet right here, five years to the day," Oley had said. He had been a small, wiry man then, his spade beard gray-shot, his eyes a bright agate blue. He had been the leader of the gang, older and more experienced—and the deadliest with a hip gun.

Cory remembered that he and Voss Grant had been the youngest members of the bunch—and Voss had topped him by a year. Joe Seltzer had been almost as old as Oley—a quiet, taciturn sort of man. Rocky Callahan, a somewhat simple-minded farm boy, had been somewhere in between.

A wild, footloose kid, Cory had run across Oley Jones and the others and thrown in with them on that holdup out of bravado rather than

26

avarice. None of them had expected more than a few hundred dollars apiece from the robbery; the size of the haul had shaken all of them.

Pursued, hounded, frightened, they had finally managed to shake the grim posses that had dogged them by risking another kind of death in the badlands.

The money was hot. They knew they could not spend a single one of the crisp new bills without immediately attracting attention. So they had buried the money and agreed to the rendezvous at Bitter Wells.

Each of them had kept his portion of the map which located the buried mail sack. None could find it without the help of the others.

"We'll lie low until things cool off," Oley had suggested. "The holdup will have been forgotten by then. We'll come back here, if we're still alive, and pick up the money together."

It had sounded all right to Cory. But he remembered that Joe had been a little dubious. Five years sounded like a heck of a long time to wait. But Oley had been convincing, and in the end of the three of them had had a drink together in the Four Aces Saloon across the street.

He turned now and saw that it was still in business. Like the hotel, it had become more rundown with the years, and Cory wondered idly if the paunchy bartender with the mole on his nose was still serving behind the counter.

Oley Jones had left Bitter Wells first. He and Joe had watched the older man ride south. Then they had parted, a little self-consciously, at the saloon tie-rack.

"Keep healthy, kid." Joe had grinned. "See you in five years!"

Now, as he stood in front of the hotel steps, the old ghosts came crowding around Bates. Rocky Callahan with the loose, foolish grin and the big strong hands. Callahan had picked up a slug through his lungs at the holdup and died on the journey across the badlands. Voss Grant, the thin blond kid from Sioux Falls, had come through without a scratch—only to be kicked to death by his hammerhead roan the last night out.

"Knew it would happen," Oley had said indifferently. "Voss was mean to the bronc—took his moods out on the cayuse." He had pointed to the ugly spur scars on the animal's withers, the

28

old welted ridges on the roan's rump.

"Liked to use his knife on the bronc," Oley had added harshly, "when he felt bad."

Oley had shot the roan and left it beside Voss's grave. That was when the slight man had decided they had better bury the mail sack.

"We'll do it fair," he had said. "We'll bury it here and come back for it when the half-dozen posses on our tail quit looking. It's a heap of money," he had said, his blue eyes glinting coldly. "We'll give them a lot of time to forget!"

He had scowled at the dubious look on Joe Seltzer's face.

"Look at it this way, Joe. It's like we was putting the money in a bank. Five years from now we come back and split it—fifty thousand apiece. Nice to think about for the next five years, ain't it?"

"What's to stop you or me or Cory from riding back here before then an' gettin' all of it?" Joe had questioned.

Oley had grinned, showing crooked yellow teeth. There was something of the ferret in his smile, in his way of thinking.

"Not if we do it my way," he said. "It'll take

29

all three of us to find where we've buried it. All three of us!" he had repeated.

His plan had seemed foolproof. They had drawn straws to see who would start it off. Cory had won. Oley and Joe had their bandannas bound tightly over their eyes, while Cory, with the mail sack across his saddle, led their mounts.

From their starting point, a wide sandy wash backed by a sandstone cliff, Cory had headed into the tortuously gullied wasteland. He had carefully drawn his section of the map in detail, up to the point where he stopped and Oley had started off at the point where Cory had stopped. Joe had taken the last leg, and it was Joe who had buried the mail sack, with Cory and Oley standing by, blindfolded.

Joe had been carefully searched to make sure he had not hidden any or all of the money upon his person; then he, too, had been blindfolded. They had left their horses to drift and had followed on foot, blind, stumbling, until after a previously agreed interval, they had taken off their blindfolds. They found themselves lost in the country north of the big butte that had been their landmark since morning.

30

A rising wind wiped out all sign of their passage; by sundown it was blowing a vicious gale. They barely managed to stagger into Bitter Wells.

Somewhere behind them they had left one hundred and fifty thousand dollars, buried in a mail sack.

I know where to start, Cory thought, staring into the hazy distance. But Oley and Joe will have to take on from where my map ends. And only Joe can find the spot where he buried the money.

HE SIGHED THEN and picked up his bag and walked up the rickety steps to the sagging hotel veranda and paused in front of the door. The westering sun reached under the wooden awning and fell across the legs of the loungers. He felt the Mexican's black eyes on him, vaguely curious. A raw-boned man in patched levis and a torn gray vest came out of a door which advertised itself as harboring the "Justice of the Peace"; he paused and put his narrow-eyed attention on Cory. A pair of sagging gun belts seemed about to slide down over his narrow hips.

31

Cory felt the stares leveled at him. But these men were strangers. Joe was not yet there, and neither was Oley. And then he had a moment's panic, wondering if they had changed so that he would not recognize them. What if one of these staring men was Joe, or Oley, and he didn't know him? But he didn't think so. Joe he was sure he would remember. And Oley, too—the small, wiry outlaw leader could not have changed that much.

He pushed the hotel door open and walked up to the desk, where a sallow-faced man with a cast in his left eye was swatting flies with a rolled-up newspaper. Cory set the bag down at his feet and read the register. Disappointment prodded sharply at him.

None of the names on the smudged page was that of one of his expected companions!

He saw that he would be the first man to register there in more than a week. Unconsciously Cory glanced at the clock above the counter. Three o'clock. This was the day, he thought anxiously. This *was* May seventeenth. But he asked the clerk just to make sure.

"Shore," the man answered negligently.

"Thursday the seventeenth." He added bitterly: "Just another day in this flea-bitten town. Why?"

Cory shrugged. "Had an appointment with someone—guess he hasn't shown up."

"Staying long?"

"Don't know," Cory muttered. "Maybe not more than tonight." He put his two dollars down on the counter and started to pick up the key the clerk tossed to him. He brought his hand across his jaw, feeling the bristle under his palm.

"Is there a barber in town?"

"Sure—four doors down the street, just past the Justice of the Peace's place," the clerk said. "Look out if Tony's quiet, though."

Cory frowned. "Why?"

"Means he's drunk," the clerk replied. "Sliced a piece off Nick Kenton's nose a few days ago. Generally has a fight with his wife about this time of the week and takes it out by belting the mescal bottle. Darn good barber when he's sober, though," the clerk added cheerfully.

"Thanks," Cory muttered. He started to pick up his bag, and the clerk leaned over the counter and stopped him. "Tony'll be closing in about

33

twenty minutes. Always closes early on Thursday. I'll take your bag up to your room for you."

Cory nodded. "Thanks again,"

He found Tony to be a short, mild-looking Mexican who chattered a little too much, but this reassured Cory.

"Not many *estranjeros* come to Bitter Wells," Tony said. "You the first in ten days, *señor*."

"You sure?" Cory asked. "No one else arrived in town today?"

"*Si.*" Tony nodded emphatically, waving his razor. "You the only one. Mister Springer from Caldwell Junction—he drive you here, no?" At Cory's absent-minded nod, "Hah, no one comes into Bitter Wells I don't see."

That meant none of the others had yet arrived. Cory looked out into the wide street, where the sun glared up from the tawny earth.

A one-horse town stuck in a corner of southern Arizona. Population fifty, counting the stray dogs that nosed in the alleys. A saloon, a general store, the "hotel" and a score of lesser ramshackle structures.

A watering place for the riders of the big Crosshatch spread and the few scattered farmers

34

further down the valley. A tawdry gateway to nowhere. . . .

They have to show up! he thought bleakly. Panic made a sharp stab again. *If they didn't—?*

He thought of the money buried out there. He'd never find it without them. Five bitter years gone for nothing!

He left the barbershop and walked back along the walk. A slight breeze ruffled the yellow neckerchief at his sun-browned throat. He sucked in his lips, feeling alone and watched. He knew the entire population of Bitter Wells was wondering what had brought him there.

A vague uneasiness came to him; he paused and looked back down the street, following it with his gaze until it became a trail which wandered off across the flats. He slid his hand down over the bone handle of his Colt, but it offered him little comfort.

"They'll be here!" he muttered. But he was no longer sure. *They've got to show up!* he thought savagely.

The desk clerk was not in sight as he went inside. There was no one in the dingy lobby, and as he went up the stairs to the second floor, the lobby clock struck four.

"Maybe they forgot the day," he told himself. "Or maybe I'm wrong. Maybe it was the eighteenth."

But he knew he was right—and he knew they had not forgotten. He walked past his door before he realized it. He turned back and put his hand on the glazed knob. Without knowing why, he hesitated.

He heard no sound to alert him. Only his own heavy brathing rasped in the silence.

"Getting real jittery," he muttered, and felt a stab of self-contempt. He turned the knob and stepped inside his room.

The man sitting on the bed was facing the door. He had a faded Army blanket wrapped around his Colt. Even so, the .45 made a sound, a muffled, heavy report, and a wisp of smoke curled up from the charred wool. The acrid odor added its pungent touch to the bite of gunsmoke.

Cory sagged in the middle. He died hard. His eyes bulged in his head and his mouth worked. He fought to get his tongue to obey his will. His fingers had closed automatically over the bone handle of his Colt, but he lacked the strength

36

to lift it.

He was still alive, however, when the killer bent over him and ran eager fingers through his pockets, looking for the map.

Cory died then, with a strangely twisted smile on his lips. Somewhere back in the past, because of doubts, built up slowly, accumulated through the years, he had prepared for just such a thing as this. . . .

The killer found no map on Cory. He searched desperately, scattering Cory's clothes about the room, dissecting every bit of Cory's personal belongings.

If Cory Bates still had his map, he had not brought it with him. The killer stood over the dead man, frustrated. . . . He had been sure Cory would have the map on him.

Somewhere out in the hallway he heard a door open. A woman's querulous voice snapped: "I'm sure I heard a shot, Henry." A man's voice came from inside the woman's room, calling her back. . . . After a moment the door closed.

The killer took a deep breath, then crossed to the door, opened it a crack and looked out. The hallway was empty. He turned and looked back at Cory's body.

"I can wait, Cory," he said softly. "I've waited five years. . . ."

He went out then, closing the door quietly behind him.

— III —

— GIRL ON THE ROAD —

WES MARTIN heard the dog barking before he came in sight of the accident on the trail. Wes had come upon the wagon road in the late afternoon, after a long ride in from the nearest rail town, and he had been pushing his horse hard.

He had left the main road at the county seat, after asking directions to Bitter Wells and receiving only vague and indefinite replies that it was somewhere on the edge of the Soapstone badlands.

It was lonely country west of the county seat— a seemingly empty expanse of sparse grass, scrub oak and thorn brush; a hard and bitter land broken by buttes and mesas. Although Wes saw

39

few signs of cattle along the way, he knew that not too many miles south were located the big Crosshatch spread and a half-dozen smaller outfits strung out along the Sweetwater. Several times, however, he spotted bands of wild mustangs dusting the low hills.

A brutal sun slammed heat down out of a cotton-flecked sky. Sweat plastered Wes' faded blue shirt to the small of his back and made half-moons under his arms. He was riding against time, and he had a rendezvous to keep for a dead man. The ex-Army scout glanced at the lowering sun with hard impatience.

Running across the little used road which was little more than a pair of wagon ruts, he had guessed which way to turn. The excited barking of the dog had turned him in that direction. Now, as he came around a sandstone outcropping flanking the road, he saw the overturned buggy.

Wes reined in. A wire-haired terrier was running back and forth in front of the overturned vehicle. The still spinning wheel indicated to Martin that the accident must have occurred only a few moments before. A line-backed dun gelding, harness trailing, was cropping spiky grass a dozen feet away.

The scout's gaze searched for the buggy driver. He saw a levis-clad, boyish figure standing shakily just beyond the vehicle. The driver must have spotted Wes at the same time; he started at a stumbling run for the buggy.

Wes kneed his rangy mount toward the overturned rig.

The slim figure ducked under the buggy and came into sight again, holding a short-barreled carbine. Close up Wes saw that the driver was a girl or a woman. The boyishness disappeared as he noticed the rounded hips and the swelling figure beneath the cotton shirt. A straw hat, wide-brimmed to shade her face, was tilted back, and Wes noticed that her hair was golden brown and had a high sheen.

He noticed, too, the hostility in her eyes.

Wes eased back in the saddle. "Need help?"

The girl shook her head, her mouth tightening. She had a scratch on her cheek, and sand still clung to the left side of her face and her left arm. She looked over twenty; in that country, old enough to be married and have two or three kids. Yet there was a quick clean look about her that made Wes think she was not wearing any man's brand.

"Not from your kind!" she snapped.

Martin slowly knuckled his two-day stubble, knowing he presented a rather dubious appearance to the girl. He was still wearing the nondescript clothes of the Army scout, a soiled, fringed buckskin jacket. And the Colt thonged down on his hip was not for decoration. Nor was the knife in the sheath at his belt.

"Glad you weren't hurt," he said, disregarding the carbine in her hands. He put his glance on the road and saw where the buggy had come down the trail and run over a rock imbedded in the roadway.

"You must have been moving pretty fast not to have seen it," he commented. "Looks like you're in a bit of a hurry."

"Whether I am or not is none of your business!" the girl retorted. Her eyes were gray, with flecks of gold dancing inside them.

Wes reappraised her, noticing the litheness and grace with which she held herself. The clothes she was wearing, though, looked as if they might belong to her brother—if she had a brother.

They were a bit loose at the waist, but tight across the buttocks. And the shirt was tight in the place where it would not be tight on her brother.

She looked outdoorsy, as though she had been born and brought up in that kind of country. But her speech and bearing somehow gave this the lie.   ,

Wes shrugged. "Sorry. I guess it isn't my business, at that." He touched fingers to his hat. "I'm a stranger to this country and—" he smiled ironically—"I seem to be lost ma'am. Or is it miss?"

"That, too, is none of your bnsiness!" she snapped. She kept the carbine muzzle on him, but there was a trace of impatience in her expression, and she bit her lips.

He nodded. "I'm headed for Bitter Wells. If you'll point out the way, I'll quit bothering you."

"It's that way," she said quickly, giving a quick tilt with her head down-trail. "About five miles."

The terrier had quit barking. He stood by her side, eyeing Wes, his head cocked to one side, his tongue out.

43

Wes swung off the sorrel. "Least I can do, ma'am," he murmured, ignoring the girl's sharp exclamation and threatening shift of muzzle. He reached down, and his shoulder muscles bunched as he righted the buggy. He crouched to examine the wheel which had run over the rock.

"Cracked the axle," he said, pointing it out. "It might hold you until you get town. But I'd take it easy on the way in."

He moved away from her, walking slowly toward the line-backed dun, who turned his head and eyed Wes with suspicion.

"Easy, fella," Wes said softly. "We'll get you hitched up in no time."

The girl watched while Martin backed the gelding between the shafts and hitched up, looping the reins around the whip handle.

Wes turned to her. "Might as well do the job right," he said dryly. "Now if you'll allow me, ma'am—"

The girl took a step backward. "Keep away from me!" she said tensely. "I can manage without—"

She didn't see him move. But the carbine was suddenly in his hands. He calmly placed the rifle

44

on the buggy seat and turned back to her. She stood stiffly, her face white. He picked her up and set her in the buggy.

The terrier growled and made a lunge for Wes' leg. The Army scout scooped him up with a careless swift gesture and deposited him beside the girl. He stepped away from the buggy and waved.

"Ride easy, ma'am." He grinned.

HE PASSED HER on the road and came into Bitter Wells when the sun was almost gone behind the shouldering bulk of Tortilla Buttes. Wes saw the town as a dirty splotch in the middle of the road. The trail ran through it and beyond it, losing itself against the dun-colored uplands to the north.

It was a wide place in a little traveled road— nothing more. But if Joe Seltzer, the man who had died in the rocks five hundred miles away, was to be believed, the key to a hundred and fifty thousand dollars was there . . . in a rendezvous Wes Martin was keeping for him.

The Army scout sat the saddle of his tired sorrel and let his hard gaze take in the town.

45

And he knew that every eye in Bitter Wells was watching him. It was that kind of a town.

The adobe-walled, two-storied Mesa House with its double-decked gallery and the saloon facing it across the street were the only two buildings of any consequence; the rest were a straggle of tin-roofed shacks.

A couple of broncs stood hipshot in front of the saloon rack. A Chinese, dressed in a black silk coat, his queue touching his shoulders, came out to the walk and emptied a bucket of slops into the street.

These were the only signs of life in Bitter Wells.

Wes glanced at the sun. He was late, but it was still the seventeenth. And somewhere in town, two men were waiting for Joe Seltzer.

Wes' grin was tight. He knew one sure way to find them. . . .

Ball's Stables were on the edge of town. Two old wagons, weathered beyond repair, decorated the manure-littered yard. Beyond the sagging-roofed barn a pole corral dipped down into a sandy wash. A couple of dispirited, sway-backed broncs stood at the far end of the enclosure, watching time and their youth fade in the shadows of the distant hills.

Wes dismounted at the foot of the wooden ramp. The big sliding door was all but closed. He waited for a moment to see if anyone would come out. A mangy tomcat with a chewed-up left ear came around the corner of the barn and flattened at the sight of Wes. The scout flipped a chunk of dirt at the cat and watched him disappear in the direction from which he had come.

He led his sorrel up the ramp and put his shoulder to the door. Rusty hinges squealed harshly in the evening quiet.

The sorrel suddenly snorted and jerked at his reins, and Wes whirled. He took a long breath and held it, eyeing the gun in the youngster's hand!

The boy was less than five feet away, inside the barn. He looked as though he had been on the way out when Wes slid the door back. But there was straw clinging to his clothes, which were, except for his hat, exact duplicates of those worn by the girl Wes had encountered on the trail. He looked like the girl, too, though his hair was lighter and cropped close, and he wore

47

his Stetson far back on his head.

"Not this time, mister!" the boy snarled. "I got a gun in my hand this time—"

"Not this time or any other time," Wes agreed. It was gloomy inside the barn, but not so dark he couldn't see that the boy must have taken a beating recently. His face was swollen, and his left eye was almost closed.

"Big Mack couldn't finish it!" the boy said bitterly. "Bettes send you in his place."

"Jeff! Jeff!" A man moved out of the deeper shadows behind the boy. "Hold your tongue, boy! He doesn't look like one of Bettes' riders to me!"

"Looks like a gunslinger to me!" the boy snarled. "And they're the only kind riding for Bettes!"

The man put a hand on Jeff's shoulder, pulling him back. "Put that gun away, Jeff. Get back out of sight. It'll be dark in an hour. You can ride home then."

Jeff stood a stubborn moment, not wanting to give ground. Waiting, Wes caught the odor of peppermint on the boy's breath. Then Jeff shrugged. He slid his Remington .44 into his

48

low-slung holster, flung a darkly hostile glance at Wes and moved away.

"I'm Ball Hotchkiss," the older man said bluntly, turning to Wes. He held a rusted single-barrel shotgun in the crook of his arm, but he made no threatening move with it. He was a short, paunchy man in his middle forties, bald, somewhat jowly. Time had seamed hard lines around his thin-lipped mouth; his eyes were gray and cold and watchful.

"The boy's had a bad time. Bunch of hoss thieves ran off some of his father's stock. He came to town an' ran afoul of Big Mack an' shot off his mouth, naming Big Mack as one of the thieves." He made a quick gesture with his free hand. "I'm telling you this, fella, so you'll understand why the kid was touchy just now."

"Don't blame him," Wes Martin said. "Wouldn't be in a welcoming mood myself, if it happened to me."

Hotchkiss nodded. His eyes were measuring Wes, taking mental note of this new man who had come to Bitter Wells. Wes looked big enough, and rawhide tough, and he reflected that Big Mack would have a rough time with

49

him, if it came to that.

"Not many strangers come to Bitter Wells," he observed. "One-hoss town way off the main roads—"

"Suits me fine," Wes cut in. He glanced toward the darkened stalls. The boy had vanished somewhere in the darkness.

The stableman shrugged. He reached out for the sorrel's bridle. "I'll take care of him. You aiming to stay in Bitter Wells for a spell?"

"Depends," Wes answered shortly. Then: "That kid with the bruised face looks like someone I know. What did you say his name was?"

"Jeff Steele." The stableman scowled. "Lives with his sister and his folks on a hoss spread on the south side of Tortilla Butte. The Drag 7. 'Bout ten, eleven miles out of town, heading east."

Wes shrugged. "Don't recall the name. Guess it was someone else."

Hotchkiss nodded. "Easy to make that kind of mistake." He indicated the near stall. "I charge a dollar day—hard money. I sleep light, and I keep a load in old Betsy here. I'm not worried you'll skip town without paying me, mister, but—"

Wes grinned. "The name's Joe Seltzer," he said. He brought out a sliver cartwheel and tossed it to the man. "Sleep easy, Ball."

Hotchkiss' fingers closed tight around the silver dollar. He heard Jeff Steele stir in the darkness at the far end of the barn. Ball licked his lips. The coin dug hard into his palm, but he was unaware of it.

— IV —

— WARNING —

WES MARTIN paused by the sagging board fence fronting the street to get his bearings. The stables were at the south end of Bitter Wells' only real street, and there was a wide, can-littered lot between it and the nearest building.

The buggy was just wheeling past him. The girl sat stiffly on the seat, the terrier beside her, his ears cocked alertly. Wes waved good-naturedly to her, but she ignored him.

He watched her drive on down the deserted street and pull in by the Mesa House. The sun was gone from the sky, and the desert purple of twilight lay over the land. Supper smells were in the air. From within one of the adobe huts at that end of town, a child suddenly began a loud bawling.

Wes measured the town. A man with a good arm could heave a rock clear to the other side of Bitter Wells.

He was not a man used to luxury or to cities, but the thought that he would not be in Bitter Wells long gave a lift to his spirits.

It occurred to him that neither Oley Jones nor Cory Bates would be pleased when he joined them. But he had Joe Seltzer's portion of the map . . . and he reflected grimly that a Colt .45, handled efficiently, puts up a powerful argument.

Wes hit the boardwalk in front of the first building and started toward the Mesa House. The girl had left her buggy, he saw, and disappeared inside some building (he was not sure which). The terrier remained on the buggy seat, eyeing the town.

Across the street loomed the Aces High Saloon. Two men came through the batwings and climbed into saddle of the horses waiting at the rack. They wheeled away from the saloon and came jogging down the street, passing Wes. The blocky, hard-faced rider on the inside gave him only a casual glance. But the man on the big bay turned and looked back at Wes with sudden interest.

Wes had a glimpse of a narrow, pockmarked face, but the rider touched no chord of recognition in him. They may have brushed elbows in some other town, long ago—but if they had Wes had forgotten.

The terrier barked sharply at him as he came abreast of the Mesa House, and he turned and grinned at the dog. "Glad you remembered me," he murmured.

He started to turn into the hotel when he heard the saloon batwings creak again. The back of Wes' neck prickled with a cold warning. He put his warbag down slowly and reached for his Bull Durham sack, and as he spun himself a cigaret, he turned slightly and send a casual glance at the man who had come out of the saloon and stood watching him.

He was a long-shanked, rangy hombre with a face shadowed by the down-tilted brim of a dirty Stetson. Something metallic glittered on the left flap of his unbuttoned vest.

Wes felt the man's long, studied regard; he

wondered if he was Oley Jones or Cory Bates. He
started to cup a match flame to his cigaret when
he heard the girl's voice, sharp across the evening
quiet, and he turned and saw her come out of
the doorway next to the hotel.

A man laughed impolitely, and she whirled
to face the doorway, her temper flaring.

"I know Jeff came to see you this morning!
You can't deny that, Mister Bettes!"

A short, grizzled man appeared in the doorway
now. Wes' glance took in the legend nailed to the
wall above him: "Dave Bettes, Justice of the
Peace." He was a thin, unkempt man in a soiled
Prince Albert coat and black stovepipe hat. A
badger beard was stained brown around the
mouth and chin with tobacco juice.

Bettes shifted his tobacco wad around in his
cheek and spat carelessly across the boards. His
eyes were like small gray chips of glass, measuring the girl with unchivalrous insolence.

"And I say you've got a hard head, Miss
Steele. I told you plain out I didn't see your
brother today. Sure, I heard he came to my office.
But I was out. I heard he walked across the
street to the saloon and got drunk and picked a

fight with Big Mack." The man's yellow-stained teeth showed in a wolfish grin. "Got beat up for his pains, too—"

"Jeff doesn't drink!" the girl cut in sharply. "And you know why he came to town. We lost fifteen more horses two days ago. One of them was my red roan mare. Jeff trailed them to that so-called horse ranch you've got hidden up by Dry Creek!"

"If your brother told you that, he's a liar!" Dave snapped. "None of my men stole your horses!"

"Jeff said they did—and I believe him!" the girl flared. "You run things pretty much your way out here, don't you? Half the men you have riding for you wouldn't dare show their faces at the county seat—"

"You making an accusation, Miss Steele?" Bettes interrupted. His eyes had a hard glint.

"I'm warning you that if Jeff's been hurt, I'll see that the law is notified. And I don't mean that gun-happy killer you pinned your badge on, either!"

The long-shanked man wearing the badge came across the street behind the girl, his boots sliding through the thick dust. He reached the boardwalk beside the buggy and stepped up, his movement quick.

He took hold of the girl's arm before she realized he was beside her.

"You shore make a lot of noise, Miss Steele!" he said harshly. "I could hear yuh disturbing the peace all the way across the street!"

The girl jerked her arm free of his grasp and whirled on him. The terrier on the buggy seat growled a low warning.

"You'll hear me a lot clearer, Vic," she snapped defiantly, "if you put a hand on me again!"

The man with the badge grinned crookedly. He was facing Wes, looking over the girl's shoulder, and his yellow-green eyes were narrowed, judging this stranger to Bitter Wells, challenging his intentions.

"I might do just that," he said insolently. He put his hands on her shoulders, and his fingers tightened. The girl cried out with a gasp of pain.

Wes Martin flipped his cigaret butt into the street. He was a man not inclined to look for trouble, and the last thing he wanted was to get

57

involved in someone else's affairs here.

But he never had been able to stand a man who hurt a woman . . . and looked him in the eye while doing it.

He said mildly: "Take your hands off her, Deputy!"

Vic's eyes glittered. "Forget it, mister. This ain't any of your business!"

Wes put his glance briefly on the sloppy man in the Prince Albert coat who was watching, with an amused smile, from the doorway.

He was one fine specimen of a justice of the peace, Wes reflected.

The girl was struggling to break loose from the deputy. As Wes stepped forward, her eyes flashed to him, bright with anger.

"You stay out of this!" she flared at him. "I can take care of myself!"

And to prove it, she kicked the rangy deputy in the shins.

Vic's teeth showed in a pained, surprised snarl. He raised his left hand and cuffed the girl on the side of the head, sending her staggering off the walk.

He was facing Martin then, his right hand

58

reaching for his Colt in anticipation of Wes' intervention, when Wes' shoulder rammed him against the building. The Army scout's body pinned the deputy's gun hand against his side; the man tried to jerk away and bring his Colt into the clear.

Wes caught his gun arm and spun him away from the wall. His own Colt made an abrupt appearance then, jamming hard into the deputy's mid-section. The man folded like a jackknife, his eyes rolling. . . .

Wes stepped back and glanced at the sloppy man in the doorway. Dave Bettes eyed the muzzle of Wes' Colt and slowly let his hand fall away from the shoulder holster under his coat. He lifted his palm to his grizzled chin and rubbed his stained beard with speculative patience.

He said softly: "You shouldn't have done that, fella. Vic ain't gonna like it."

"Never thought much of a man who'd hit a woman," Wes replied. "He's welcome to make what he wants of this."

He took his gaze off Bettes and noticed with faint surprise that the girl was gone. In the excitement he had not heard the buggy wheel away.

Now he put his glance down the shadow-filled street in time to see her turn into Ball's stable yard.

He smiled wryly. She had not even bothered to see what had happened. He felt a cynical amusement at this. Evidently she and her brother were quite a pair.

Bettes had followed his glance. "You work for the Steeles?"

Wes shook his head and holstered his Colt. "I'm on vacation," he said, and there was faint irony in his voice.

Bettes frowned. "Then you better keep out of Vic's way, if you want to enjoy it. Better yet, clear out of Bitter Wells."

Wes shrugged. "Might just take that advice, Mr. Bettes," he agreed: "I didn't come here to stay."

"Few do," Bettes nodded. "If I was you, I'd be gone by morning."

"That's just the trouble," Wes said easily, prodding his forefinger against Dave's chest. "Too many people wish they were somewhere else. It ain't healthy."

He turned on his heel, leaving the dirty figure

60

staring after him. . . . He picked up his war-bag, and he was smiling as he entered the lobby of the Mesa House.

THE DESK CLERK was trimming the wick on his lamp when the Army scout loomed over the counter. He set the glass chimney carefully in place and turned to appraise the big man with the campaign hat thumbed back from his forehead.

"By the week, or just for the night?" the clerk asked routinely, turning the register around toward Wes.

"Don't know yet," Wes replied. He ran his rorefinger down the inked names on the page. "I'm expecting to meet a friend of mine here today," he explained. "Two of them, in fact."

The clerk pursed his lips. He was a thin, serious-minded young man who had been born with a club foot and abandoned as a baby. He had been with Tom Vesey, owner of the hotel, since Tom and his wife had found him in the wicker basket beside the stream that in the rainy season ran in the gully behind the house.

He looked Wes over again, remembering Cory

Bates' questions a few hours earlier. He nodded crisply.

"Only other stranger in town checked in about two this afternoon. His name's—" He glanced at the register, reading the signature under Wes' forefinger. "That's the man. Cory Bates."

"That's him." Wes nodded. "Him and Oley Jones were to meet me here. Sort of a reunion, you might call it."

The clerk smiled primly. "Mr. Bates is in room 211. He was expecting you. He mentioned a Mr. Jones and a Mr. Seltzer—"

"I'm Joe Seltzer," Wes answered evenly.

"No Mr. Jones has checked in yet," the clerk said. "But I saw Mr. Bates go up to his room more than an hour ago."

Wes nodded and placed a silver dollar on the register beside the Joe Seltzer signature with which he had signed in. "That's for you," he said. "When Mr. Jones shows up, send him right along. We'll be in Room 211, waiting for him."

He picked up his warbag and crossed the dingy lobby to the palm-shrouded stairs.

As Wes disappeared upstairs, Dave Bettes came into the lobby. He leaned against the counter and eyed the stairs, picking at his teeth with a sliver toothpick. A small frown puckered his grizzled brows.

"Cool hombre, that one, Kenny," he muttered. "Second stranger to come to town in one day." He shook his head. "It ain't usual for Bitter Wells." He turned to the desk clerk. "What did he want?"

"He asked about a Cory Bates and an Oley Jones. Said they were old friends of his who had planned a reunion here."

Bettes whistled softly. "Reunion, eh? Here?" He made a short sound of disbelief through his lips. "Looked more like one of Quantrill's old riders, if you ask me. Did you catch his name?" Kenny nodded. "He said he was Joe Seltzer."

Bettes sucked his lips in over his snaggled teeth. "Never heard of him. But this is my town, Kenny. And I don't like strange gunmen coming into it. Don't like it at all!"

BATES' ROOM was at the far end of the dimly lighted hallway. Boards creaked under Wes' boots as he rounded the newel post on the second floor and put his glance down the gloomy pas-

63

sageway.

A window faced the hall at the back of the hotel. Under it was a rickety landing and a flight of stairs leading to a back yard. It was a fire exit to be used by the upstairs tenants. The window was open now, and a faint breeze churned the day's close heat. . . .

Wes paused. He heard a murmuring of voices from the lobby, and he thought he recognized Bettes' tone. He smiled faintly. The man was suspicious. And remembering the Steele girl's accusations, he decided Dave Bettes probably had a right to be. Wes shrugged. He was not in Bitter Wells to check on Dave Bettes.

He was there to pick up fifty thousand dollars that belonged to Joe Seltzer and which—in a way—had been willed to him.

Wes knew that Cory would immediately know he was not Joe Seltzer. What Bates would do when Wes confronted him would depend on what kind of a man he was, and how much the money meant to him.

Going down the hallway, he heard the drunken snoring of some occupant in the room near the head of the stairs. A little farther on, a woman's nasal tones came through the thin door panels. "I did hear a shot, Sam—don't you dare tell me I didn't! About an hour ago, while you were out, probably swilling that cheap whiskey they serve across the street—"

A floor board popped under Wes' feet, and the woman's voice was cut off abruptly. Silence prevailed behind the door. Wes walked on to Bates' room close by the back window and knocked. He waited, listening for Bates behind the door. The breeze coming in through the window at his elbow brought the odor of chile and the sudden snarling cry of a cat momentarily trapped by a prowling dog.

A door opened midway up the hallway, and Wes turned his head, laying his quick glance on the whiskered, stumpy man who had cautiously stuck his head out. This was obviously the husband of the woman whose voice he had heard in passing. The man stared at him with bright suspicion, then slowly pulled back inside and closed the door.

Behind Bates' door was an empty stillness.

Wes knocked again. The clerk had been definite about the fact that Bates was in his room.

65

But there was a strange lack of movement, and Wes tensed warily as he put his hand on the knob, turned it and shoved the door open.

Inside the room was a smothering blackness. He saw nothing move, nor was he greeted. Wes dropped his warbag and took two steps inside, and then he heard faint, mocking laughter from his left and spun around, drawing his Colt.

He caught a faint smell of peppermint in the room and as he whirled he stumbled over a body on the floor. It threw him off balance and into the unseen clubbed Colt wielded by a shadowy assailant.

He didn't feel the impact as he hit the floor.

— V —

— PRESSURE — BITTER WELLS STYLE —

WES MARTIN felt the light against his eyes
first on regaining consciousness. He rolled over
and lay face up, watching the scabrous ceiling
wheel slowly in a lopsided rhythm. His thoughts
pulled together, like the pieces of a pupzle, and
as he began to remember what had happened,
he heard Vic's harsh voice jeer: "I told you he
had a tough skull, Dave. He's coming to."

The Army scout lay quiet, trying to still the
revolving ceiling. There was a sharp pain over his
left ear and a dull throbbing in his head. Finally
he turned and looked at the speaker.

Bitter Wells' special deputy sat on the edge
of the bed, his hat cocked back on his balding

head. He had a Colt in his hand, held idly. A sneer spread across his wedge-shaped features as he saw Wes' attention focus on him.

Between Wes Martin and the deputy lay a dead man. He was curled up in a ball, his knees pulled up against his chest—a big, gaunt man with a freshly shaved face.

Martin had the sinking feeling that the dead man was Cory Bates.

He started to get up on his hands and knees, and the deputy got up off the bed and put a heavy boot down between Wes' shoulders and shoved. Wes sprawled face down and rolled over, his anger overriding the throbbing pain in his head. He lunged to his feet, and his right hand reached instinctively for his Colt. He brushed the top of his empty holster and stopped short, eyeing the deputy's gun muzzle, which was leveled ominously at his belt buckle.

Dave Bettes' voice was mild. "Vic's just begging for an excuse, fella."

Wes Martin took a deep breath. "I'll be." His eyes were narrowed, watchful.

Vic chuckled. "Real tough hombre," he said, baiting Wes. "Assaults the law as soon as he comes to town. Ten minutes later he's in a room with a dead man—"

"Just a minute!" Wes snapped. "I didn't kill him. If you'll check my gun, you'll see it hasn't been fired!"

Dave nodded. "It's been checked. We know you didn't kill him. Fact is, we don't care who did. Never saw the jasper in Bitter Wells before." He shrugged, as though the whole thing didn't matter much.

"It's just that we like to keep our town clean, mister. We don't like gunmen riding in to settle private grudges."

"It wasn't that kind of a meeting," Wes muttered. He could see the logic of the man's reasoning, but he was faintly suspicious of his motives.

"We checked the register and talked with Kenny, the desk clerk," Bettes said. "You told him you were Joe Seltzer and you wanted to see Cory Bates. Why?"

"I had an appointment with him here today." Wes' voice was tight. "Me, Bates and Oley Jones. We agreed to meet here in Bitter Wells—"

"What for?" Vic interrupted harshly.

"That's our business!" Wes answered grimly.

69

Bettes shook his head. "Where's this other fella, Jones?"

Wes shrugged. "Far as I know, he hasn't showed up yet."

The deputy toed the dead man. "Someone killed Bates. You reckon it was this Jones jasper, Dave?"

"Maybe," Dave said. "But I doubt it." He turned to Wes. "There ain't a flea that can crawl into Bitter Wells without everybody in town knowing it. And you and this fella Bates are the only strangers to come to town in ten days."

Wes Martin glanced around the hotel room. It was a shabby, meagerly furnished hole-in-the-wall, a sorry place to die in. But someone had known Bates would be showing up today and had waited there to kill him. Only Jones could have known. And yet, according to these two men, no one answering Jones' description had come to Bitter Wells.

Bettes was fingering his dirty beard. "Now I'll tell *you* what is bothering me," he said coldly. "Three men held up the stage and took the express box about four days ago. The sheriff was out looking for the holdup men; he and a posse came through here two days ago. He reckoned they might have tried to cross the Soapstones into New Mexico."

Wes eyed him warily. "What's that got to do with me?"

"Three men!" Dave Bettes emphasized the number, his voice ominous. "The driver said he heard one of them call another Joe Seltzer!"

Wes fought the sinking feeling in his stomach. "That driver was lying. Or those holdup men were trying to frame me!"

"Frame you?" Bettes mocked. "How?"

Wes' mouth set harshly. He had come there as Joe Seltzer, and he knew he'd have to play his role out. It was to have been a simple job. But now Cory Bates was dead and Oley Jones had not shown up. And, he reflected grimly, a hundred and fifty thousand dollars buried somewhere in the badlands northwest of town could draw a lot of flies. . . .

"The sheriff is due back through here tomorrow," Bettes said softly. "I reckon I could forget your name if you'd tell me what you came to Bitter Wells for."

"It was just a reunion," Wes muttered, "between friends."

Bettes scowled. His eyes turned hard and flat-looking, like gray slate.

"All right, fella. You tell that story to the sheriff in the morning. Try convincing him you and your friends were just planning a little convention in town."

Vic prodded Wes and made a motion with his Colt. "In the meantime we've got just the room for you, Joe. Not as fancy as this one, mebbe— but it's free. Pick up your warbag you left in the hall and let's get going. I'm anxious to check you in."

Wes did as he was told. He walked ahead of Vic and Dave Bettes, going down the hallway. A hatchet-faced woman and her stumpy husband peered at him as he went by their door. He heard her mutter: "I told you I heard a shot—"

He walked down the stairs and across the dingy lobby, and he kept thinking of the faint peppermint odor that had been in Bates' room. And he knew that Jeff Steele had been the man behind the clubbed Colt. It looked as though Jeff had killed Cory Bates. And Wes wanted to know why. He wanted desperately to know where Jeff

Steele figured in this rendezvous that had mis-
fired!

THE BITTER WELLS jail was a bare back
room in Dave Bettes' office. It was furnished with
a wobbly cot and a straw pad and an old Army
blanket. A wooden box provided extra seating
capacity. A tin can still held the shredded butts
of the former inmates; the floor was dirty, and
cobwebs showed up in the corners where the
lamplight reached.

Wes Martin's pockets had been emptied in the
office. Vic stood by while he performed the task.
The deputy's eyes watched Wes as he placed
matches, change, money and a pocket knife on the
desk. Dave Bettes then took Vic's Colt and stood
by while the deputy went over Wes carefully
from behind. He found Wes' sheath knife, eyed
it for a moment, then tossed it on the table beside the other items.

"Reckon that's all," he said, looking at Dave.
" 'Bout forty-two dollars on him. Just enough
for a good three-day drunk."

Dave swept the items into the top drawer of
his desk. "You'll get this back in the morning,

when the sheriff takes you off my hands," he muttered. He made a motion toward the cell. "It's all yours, fella."

Wes walked into the bare room, and the door shut hard behind him. He heard a key turn in the lock. He walked to the cot now hidden in the darkness, felt it against his shins and sat down. There was a stale, unwashed odor in the room.

Wes Martin considered his predicament. He had come there as Joe Seltzer, expecting trouble, if any, only from Cory Bates and Oley Jones. In the morning he would have to explain his presence to the sheriff, and it occurred to him that the local lawman would not take kindly to his explanation. At best he could expect a long sojourn in the cell while the lawman checked back on his identity; at worst, the sheriff would not believe him.

He stood up and paced restlessly, ignoring the throbbing in his head.

Someone had the section of map Joe Seltzer had given him. He couldn't know if Bettes or his special deputy, Vic, had taken it while he was lying unconscious in Cory Bates' room, or if Jeff Steele had gone through his pockets first.

74

But he no longer had Joe's map, and it meant, oddly enough, that the Steele boy must have known of the rendezvous. This bothered Wes. Joe had been clear about one thnig: only he, Cory and Oley Jones knew of the money buried in the badlands outside of town.

It could be that Jeff had found the buckskin pouch containing the map in his pocket and taken it more out of curiosity than understanding.

But what had brought the belligerent youngster to Cory's room in the first place? Jeff, he felt sure, had not killed Bates. Or if he had, he had not killed him in the few moments prior to Wes' knock on the door. For Cory Bates had looked as though he had been dead for at least an hour. . . . Wes settled back on the cot, his eyes bleak. There was a lot here that didn't make sense. A stage holdup by three men—and one of them was called Joe Seltzer by his companions. Wes knew that the real Joe Seltzer was dead. But if Seltzer had been alive and on his way to a rendezvous with Oley Jones and Cory Bates (as he would have been), then the stage holdup would have been a frameup hard to beat.

The irony of it brought a thin smile to Wes Martin's face. In thirty years of ups and downs, this was his first venture into the shadowy border just outside the law. He was a man who had always been honest with himself and with others, and he wasn't fooling himself now.

Joe Seltzer had given him fifty thousand dollars for trying to save his life, or because he was dying anyway and it was easy for him to be generous. But the money had not belonged to Joe Seltzer, and Wes knew it. Five years might have placed the robbery outside the statute of limitations, but Wes was not that well informed legally, and he had not cared.

He had seen a chance to pick up more money than he would ever earn in a lifetime, and he had put aside his principles and come to Bitter Wells to pick up what seemed an easy fortune.

But for Wes Martin, he reflected wryly, nothing ever came easy. . . .

He got to his feet again, too restless to stay put, and walked to the window. There was no glass left in it, only a strap iron latticework that looked as though it were the work of the local blacksmith. It was screwed to the wood frame.

Wes put his hands on the cold iron and tested it. The latticework was firm. He turned and walked back to the cot and forced himself to settle down.

A HALF-HOUR or so later, Wes became aware of Dave Bettes and his deputy talking in the other room. But their voices were low and the words not distinguishable. After a while he heard the outer door close, and a key was turned in the lock. Then it was quiet again in the flat-roofed, narrow building, and Wes knew that both men had gone out once more.

Wes frowned. He had no doubt that Dave Bettes was running his own game here, using his phony title as justice of the peace as a cover. Once he got wind of what Wes had come there for, there was little doubt he'd try to cut himself in on the money.

Impatience gnawed at Wes. Somehow he had to get out of this cell tonight—he had to get to Jeff Steele. It was no longer only a matter of the money. He had been slugged and framed, and he wanted to know who, and why!

It was obvious the tough Steele kid knew about the rendezvous in Bitter Wells. It was also clear that he knew more about this than anyone else in town.

Unless it was Oley Jones! Wes pondered the thought. Of the three men who were to meet in Bitter Wells, only Jones had not put in an appearance. Why?

Several possibilities presented themselves to the Army scout. Oley Jones might be dead. Or he had been delayed. That was likely. And if that was so, then Jones might be showing up within a day or two.

But if Jones had died, the loot buried in the Soapstone badlands might never be recovered. Looking at it coldly, Wes wondered why the holdup boss had ever designed such a plan. Hard-pressed and knowing that any attempt to spend that kind of money would immediately give them away, Jones had figured out the scheme of burying the loot and coming back for it later.

But there were two weak links in the plan.

One was the five-year enforced wait. A waiting period was understandable, but five years put a high premium on a man staying alive and out of jail.

78

The other was that the recovery of the buried money depended on the three of them coming back to Bitter Wells.

And Oley Jones had not come back!

Wes was about to get up again when he heard the hand brush softly against the barred window. He turned quickly in the dark, his eyes searching the window square. He saw a shadow move across the latticework, and then something metallic clanged softly.

Wes came up off the cot, as soundless as a prowling cougar. The metal object slid down the inner wall of the cell. Wes crossed to the window side and flattened himself against the cold wall, his eyes narrowed and bleakly suspicious.

A gun was being lowered into the cell at the end of a piece of twine. It came down slowly until it bumped softly against the floor. Then a face appeared, pressing against the iron latticework. . . .

Wes' right hand snaked through one of the openings. His steel-hard fingers closed around a soft throat. A startled gasp was cut off short. And he found himself looking into the face of the girl he had tried to help on the trail to Bitter Wells!

His fingers loosened and he asked bleakly:

79

"What kind of a game are you playing, Miss Steele?"

She gulped and massaged her throat for a moment. Finally her voice came in a squeaky whisper. "I thought you were asleep—"

"And you figured out a new way to awaken me," he cut in dryly. Then, harshly: "Just what are you up to?"

"I want you out," she said. As her voice gained strength, a note of defiance sounded in it. "You helped me this afternoon. I want to return the favor."

"Why?"

"I told you." She sounded desperate now. "It's my brother, Jeff. He's disappeared. I've looked all over town. I know he's in some kind of trouble. And I can't think of anyone else I can turn to for help."

He had to say it. "You didn't care for my help this afternoon, Miss Steele. I'm sorry I don't believe you now."

He started to turn away from the window. Her voice rose slightly, calling him back. "Please?" Wes looked back. "I thought you were one of Dave Bettes' new riders—" She took a deep breath. "I still don't know who you are. But it's obvious you're not working for Bettes—and you did want to help me, once—"

Wes strode back to the window. "All right, Miss Steele—I'll go along with that."

The girl breathed a sigh of relief. "This gun," she said quickly, "I borrowed it from Ball Hotchkiss." She turned her head in sudden alarm, and her voice lowered. "I've got to go now. They're coming back. I'll meet you in Ball's Stables—"

"Wait!" Wes' voice held an edge of doubt. "Are you sure that Hotchkiss can be trusted?"

"He's my father's friend," the girl said. "He knows why we came and settled here—" She withdrew hurriedly from the window, and Wes saw her dart into the thicker shadows between the two buildings. A moment later Wes heard the outer door open and close softly.

The Army scout unknotted the twine from the trigger guard of the Colt and examined the gun in the faint starshine filtering in through the barred window. He found it loaded, and it appeared to be in working order.

Yet he didn't feel right about it. He walked back to the cot, slid the twine under the pad and

81

stood frowning, trying to grasp something that nagged at him. Jeff Steele had been with Ball Hotchkiss all afternoon. Judging from his appearance, the straw still clinging to his clothes, the kid had probably slept off the results of his beating in the loft. If so, why hadn't the stableman told the girl? Or was she lying about her brother's disappearance?

The man who had come back to the law offices was now headed for the cell. Wes quickly slid the Colt under the pad and sat down, a dangerous glint in his eyes. This, too, somehow seemed too pat.

The cell door swung open. It banged gently against the inner wall, but there was no one framed in the doorway. A glint of admiration came into the Army scout's eyes. Dave Bettes was a wary old fox; his sloppy appearance belied his canniness.

Lamplight spilled a bar of illumination across the threshold, reaching as far as the edge of the cot. Dave Bettes moved into sight then, standing a good five feet inside the outer office. He was holding a cocked pistol in his right hand.

"Glad to see you wasn't trying any tricks."

82

He chuckled. "I want to talk with you, while Vic's away."

Wes said: "I've got ears," and waited.

Dave Bettes shuffled cautiously into the cell. He could see Wes sitting on the cot, and his eyes made a swift search of the room. He saw nothing amiss.

"I've been thinking things over," he said, leaning back against the cell door. "Strikes me funny that a man of your kind would fall into a trap like this. Riding into town so soon after the stage holdup—"

"You still think I'm one of the men who held up that stage?"

Dave shrugged. "Now I'm a man who believes what he hears, though not *all* he hears." His grin had a sort of obscene twist to it. He worked his chaw of tobacco around in his mouth, looked across the room and then spat on the floor.

"Never take a man at his face value, I say, or judge things by the way they look."

"Careful cuss, arent' you?" Wes said curtly.

"Have to be. This is a tough town, mister. Stuck like a wart on the edge of the Soapstone badlands. There ain't much between her and

83

Taos. Used to be a stage run through town on its way to Santa Fe. But it lost too much money. Why, there ain't any excuse for this town being here now. Sort of a watering place for the boys on the spreads south and east. But we get another breed of cat every now and then—the kind who's looking back over his shoulder and keeps a quick hand on his Colt."

He paused and Wes sensed Bettes was waiting for some remark from him. But Wes kept silent.

Dave prodded him, his grin crooked, expectant. "You heard me, mister?"

Wes nodded. "So it's a tough town," he agreed. "What are you getting at?"

"You came here to rendezvous with a couple of pals," Bettes said. "Why here? What is there in Bitter Wells to interest you?"

Wes put his hand on the edge of the cot, and his fingers slowly worked under the pad. "Might be because I'm that strange breed of cat," he said coldly. "Maybe I don't like what's on my back trail—"

"Quit stalling!" Bettes snarled. His voice was ugly now; there was little patience in it. "Let me in on why you came to Bitter Wells, and I'll see

84

that you ain't here when the sheriff rides by in the morning."

"I don't intend to be," Wes said flatly. He straightened up, and the gun in his hand caught Bettes flat-footed. "Let's just swap places for a while," he suggested grimly.

Bettes stiffened against the door framing. His gun hand quivered. But something he saw in Wes' eyes, a dangerous, unsmiling glitter, held him, forestalled any rash move on his part.

"You won't live to get out of town," he muttered. "Vic's waiting just across the street."

"I'll take my chances," Wes said. He walked to the old reprobate, took the gun from his hand and jammed it under his belt. It was a .38 Smith and Wesson with a cut-down barrel, and Wes reckoned it came from a shoulder holster under Bettes' coat. But he made Dave turn around and assured himself the man had no other weapon on him before spinning him around and shoving him toward the cot.

"All right," he growled. "Who's got it? You or Vic?"

"Got what?"

"A piece of wrapping paper about six inches

square, a penciled drawing of a map.'

Dave's yellow teeth showed in a wolfish grin. "So that's it, fella? That's why you came to town? A map?"

"No," Wes corrected him. "I had the map. Somebody took it from me up in Cory Bates' room. It was either you or Vic—"

"Or the man who slugged you!" Bettes cut in harshly. "Blast it, Joe, tell me what you're after, and I'll throw in with you! For a fifty-fifty cut—"

"You'll get a cut, across the mouth!" Wes snapped. He motioned with the gun. "Sit down. You can bellow as soon as I leave. But if you try it now, I'll have to quiet you with this!"

Bettes glowered as he sank down on the cot. "You darn fool!" he raged. "You can't get away with this in my town! If you got any sense—"

Wes closed the door on him. He turned the key in the lock and left it hanging there. He listened for a moment, smiling grimly. There was no immediate outcry from Bettes.

Turning to the desk, Wes began to go through the drawers. He found his Colt and cartridge belt and buckled it on, leaving Dave Bettes' .38 in its place. He thrust the gun the girl had lowered into the cell under his belt, stepped up to the lamp and blew it out.

He stepped outside, and still Bettes made no outcry. Wes put his hard gaze on the lighted window of the saloon across the street. If Vic was inside, why wasn't Bettes yelling his head off?

He waited for a long moment, a tall and suspicious man who was beginning to find that one hundred and fifty thousand dollars, buried ten years ago, was drawing a lot of flies.

He could say the heck with it and get out of Bitter Wells while he could—or he could stick around and find out why a girl he didn't know, and who had indicated she couldn't care less about knowing him, had suddenly decided to help him break out of jail.

He moved briskly away from the jail, keeping to the shadows. Behind him Dave Bettes was strangely silent.

— VI —

— SHOTGUN DEAL —

BALL HOTCHKISS moved restlessly away from the ramp, his narrowed gaze searching the night. The noises which drifted to him from uptown had no unusual import; he felt a crawling uneasiness disturb him. He didn't like the girl's plan, but he had agreed with her she had no other choice.

Behind him he heard the stamping of horses in their stalls. The rangy stud, particularly, seemed restless. Ball thought of the man who had ridden him into town, and a chill put goose pimples down his spine. If things didn't go off just right, they'd have a tiger by the tail!

He kept waiting for some commotion up the

street, some indication that the man who called himself Joe Seltzer had broken out of jail. After a moment he took his pipe from his pocket and clamped it between his teeth. At the moment he was glad to have something to chew on.

Where was Seltzer? Had he suspected a trap?

He heard a soft whisper from behind him and he turned, pausing just inside the glow of the turned-down lantern hanging from an overhead rafter.

The girl whispered despairingly, "Isn't he coming?"

Ball faced her. She was hidden in the deep shadows by the first stall, his shotgun in her hands. Ball had insisted she take the shotgun; it argued with a big fist at close quarters.

"Looks like he smelled a rat," Ball said. "Either he's staying put—or he's taken the chance to leave town, although I can't see him leaving that big stud behind." He shrugged. "Anyway, it don't seem like it went the way you expected it would, Miriam—"

"Things went just the way you wanted them, Miss Steele!" Wes' steel hard voice interrupted. It came from the darkness of the yard, just behind Ball. "Now if you'll just put that shotgun down and step outside to join Mr. Hotchkiss in the light, I'll feel more kindly to you!"

The girl gasped. Ball's back was ramrod stiff. He didn't look arount at Wes. He said quickly, harshly: "You better do as he says, Miriam."

The girl propped the shotgun against the stall boards and walked into the light. Only then did Hotchkiss turn to face Wes moving alertly out of the shadows.

"She didn't mean you no harm," Ball said tensely. "She just wanted a chance to talk to you—"

"I get close-mouthed in front of a shotgun muzzle," Wes cut in bleakly. "And I think you're a liar, even if you are trying to be a gentleman about it."

Hotchkiss scowled. "She got you free, didn't she?" he pointed out.

"But she doesn't trust me." The Army scout chuckled grimly. He moved by Ball and into the barn, turning quickly to get his broad shoulders against the inner wall. He was on the edge of the lantern light, a big, cold-eyed man with a gun in his hand. He made a slight motion with it.

90

"Let's all get away from the doorway," he suggested. "That special deputy of Bettes' might be out looking for me, and somebody might get hurt."

Miriam Steele moved toward him, and Ball put his shoulder to the door, closing all but a foot of the aperture. He turned to face Wes, his pipe jutting stiffly from his jaw.

"We know why you're here," the girl said hurriedly. "I don't care about the money—"

"Money?" Wes' voice was dry, probing.

"A hundred and fifty thousand dollars!" Ball snapped. "Buried around here somewhere!"

"Well, well," Wes breathed, "I didn't know it was common knowledge."

He sounded disappointed.

"It ain't!" Ball growled. "And to tell the truth, we're just guessing."

"Who's we?"

"My father, my brother and I," the girl cut in stiffly. Her voice sounded high-strung, close to tears. Wes had the feeling she wasn't so hard and mannishly capable as she appeared to be.

"Dad's willing to forget about the money," Miriam continued. "But Jeff isn't. He thinks Dad earned the money—and he wants it!"

Wes eyed her, frowning. "I don't recall any-one named Steele having a claim on that money."

The girl looked at Hotchkiss; her lips quivered as she tried to hold back her disappointment.

"I see that anything I can say will not make sense to you, Mister Seltzer," she said bitterly. "I just wanted you to know that my father and I don't feel the way Jeff does about the money. And my main interest is in seeing that my brother does not get hurt."

Wes raised an eyebrow in a gesture of disbelief.

Miriam's eyes flared in anger. "You and your friends can have the money!" she flung at him. "You all should be in jail, anyway—you stole that money in the first place—but if you hurt Jeff, I'll see that you hang for it!"

She turned and started to leave.

Wes took a step after her. "Hey," he said, "wait a minute."

She looked right through him. Her voice was brittle. "Ball—I need a horse."

Hotchkiss nodded quickly. "I'll saddle up the

92

gray mare for you, Miss Steele."

As he headed for the stalls, Wes stepped in front of Miriam, a small smile giving a rueful tilt to his lips. He pushed his hat back from his forehead and scratched his head. "I apologize, ma'am—I mean Miss Steele. I believe *you* don't care about the money—"

Her voice was icy. "Thank you, Mister Seltzer!"

His smile widened to a grin, and it was a little sheepish. "I don't know if you'll believe me now," he said, "but I'm not Joe Seltzer."

Ball Hotchkiss was halfway to the stall of the gray mare when he heard this. He paused, turning to eye Wes with a sudden frown.

The girl said: "You don't have to make up a story for me—"

"It's the truth," Wes cut in bluntly. "I came to Bitter Wells to pick up Joe's share of the money."

Miriam stared at him, disbelief still strong in her eyes.

Ball said harshly from farther down by the stalls, "If you're not Joe Seltzer, who are you?"

"The name's Wes Martin." Wes smiled a bit

ruefully. "Guess I'm a little like your brother, Miss Steele. I happen to think I earned a little of that money."

Miriam said tightly, "I don't believe you!"

Wes shrugged. "I didn't figure things would get so all-fired complicated." He sighed and pulled his wallet from his pocket. He took a folded piece of paper that was tucked in out of sight in a slit in the leather.

"My Army discharge," he said. He handed it to the girl.

She eyed him for a moment before dropping her gaze to the paper. Ball came up and peered over her shoulder.

"Looks genuine," she said. But doubt still lingered in her voice. "Why didn't you show this to Dave Bettes?"

"I wanted to show it to the sheriff," Wes said. He added dryly: "I don't trust Bettes."

Miriam smiled faintly.

"If you're not Joe, how did you know about the buried money?" Ball said grimly.

Wes looked coldly at Hotchkiss, not liking the man. "That's my business," he said.

"It's Miss Steele's business, too!"

94

Wes frowned. "Was your father in on the holdup?"

"No!" Miriam's voice was bitter now. "But the authorities claimed he was!" She forced back tears of anger. "Five men forced their way into the express car of the Santa Fe Limited five years ago, tied up the messenger and got away with one hundred and fifty thousand dollars. The messenger remembered them talking—heard the names Cory Bates and Joe Seltzer and Voss Grant. He never forgot those names, because he spent three years out of a seven-year sentence in a prison cell at the Yuma Penitentiary. Three years, Mister Hardin, although he was an innocent man. All because some zealous prosecutor made a jury believe he was in with the holdup men!"

Wes nodded. The pattern was suddenly clearer. The names Cory Bates and Joe Seltzer were known to this girl's brother—it was very possible that he had killed Bates earlier. And Wes recalled that Jeff had been in the stable and had heard Wes tell Hotchkiss he was Joe Seltzer.

"My father came to this country because of that money," Miriam went on. "He was a bitter

95

man at first. But now he's seen what that money's done to Jeff, and—" She shook her head, her eyes bright with unshed tears. "All we want is to be let alone. They can have the money. I just don't want to see Jeff mixed up in it!"

"He may already be mixed up in it," Wes said. He took her arm before she could shape a reply. "Mind if I see you home? I'd like to meet your father."

Miriam hesitated. "I came to find my brother—" She looked at Ball Hotchkiss.

"He was here earlier, like I told you," Ball said. "Had a run-in with Big Mack. I cleaned him up, and he slept for a while up in the loft." He put his suspiciius gaze on Wes. "He had just come down when you showed up, mister—"

Wes said: "And he heard me tell you I was Joe Seltzer." He eyed Hotchkiss. "Where did Jeff go then?"

"I don't know," Ball growled. "I left him here and went over to the Chink restaurant to eat. I wanted to bring him some food, but he said he didn't want any. When I got back, he was gone."

"Jeff came to Bitter Wells to see Dave Bettes," Miriam explained. "That's what he told Father. But Dad was worried. That's why I came after him. Jeff said he was sure the men who raided our stock were Bettes' men. He said he recognized Big Mack from his bulk, even though it was dark when they tore down our corral gate."

"Every shady character in the section works for Dave Bettes," Ball rasped. "He's got a ranch up Dry Creek. That's what he calls it. Hideout is a better name for it. The Crosshatch's been losing beef, but so far they haven't done much about it."

"Maybe Jeff has gone home," Wes said, trying to reassure the girl. He wanted to have a talk with the boy.

Hotchkiss nodded. "Sure," he put in. "That's probably where he is now. But if he should show up here later, I'll send him home," he promised.

Miriam said: "Thank you." She put a hand on the stableman's arm. "You're the only friend we have in town."

Ball said gruffly: "You'd better leave the buggy here. I'll see that axle gets fixed first thing in the morning." He turned away. "I'll saddle

97

that gray mare for you now."

"Prince!" the girl said suddenly. She looked around for the dog. "Where is he?"

"Somewhere around in back," the stableman said, "hunting rats. I'll take care of him for you." He made a wry gesture. "I can stand him around here for a few days, what with the rats I've been having lately. Lost two bags of grain to them just last week. . . ."

WES MARTIN and the girl rode away from Ball's Stables five minutes later. As a precaution, Ball let them out through the back gate in the corral, which put them in the shadows of the arroyo which angled southeast out of the wash. He stood by the gate and watched them vanish and was mildly surprised that no one came looking for Wes Martin.

Then he turned and walked back to the street and tried to figure out why Dave Bettes had made no fuss over Martin's escape. He didn't like it. He felt nervous, and his eyes held a wary gleam, like those of a cat backed into a corner.

He went back to his quarters and threw some cans and supplies into a gunny sack, then went into the barn and saddled the big gray mule he used whenever he left town. He rode out the same way Wes and the girl had gone, but he turned north once he got well out of town.

An hour later he was skirting the crinkled lava beds which tongued out of the badlands. He followed along the edges of this barrier for several miles, passing up numerous gullies leading back into the bleak and forbidding mass.

Finally he turned into one of the fissures, which was seemingly no different from the others. He rode slowly, following this narrow, twisting crack in the huge lava field for about a mile.

The fissure widened to a small pocket under a burnt, ugly hill. A small fire came into view only when Ball rounded the last jut of lava; he rode forward at a slow, cautious pace.

The campfire barely lightened an area ten feet in diameter. No one was in sight, but Hotchkiss rode boldly up to its glow and dismounted. He waited, looking down into the flames—a paunchy, stoop-shouldered man with a glint in his eyes.

Jeff Steele stepped out of the shadows. He came up to the fire, and his voice was edgy.

"Trouble?"

Ball shrugged. "The fella you slugged in Bates' hotel room—I think he knows it was you up there." His voice was tight. "You an' yore blasted peppermints! If you stuck to tobacco, like a man—" He broke off, making a disgusted sound.

Jeff's lower jaw jutted. "I got the map from him, didn't I? Bates was dead when I got to his room. Been dead over an hour, I'd say—shot in the stomach and chest. I searched him, but there was nothing in his pockets. Then this Joe Seltzer knocked on the door—"

"You should have killed him," Ball said harshly. "Now he knows you were there. He's going to be looking for you." His lips tightened. "He's after that money, too, Jeff!"

"To the devil with him!" Jeff snarled. "Pa spent three stinking years in that hell hole at Yuma! Three years for nothing. He worked for the Santa Fe for eleven years. And they paid him off by calling him a liar and making a scapegoat out of him." His fists tightened as he looked off into the darkness. "Pa earned that one hundred and fifty thousand dollars, Ball—and by gosh,

100

I'm going to get it for him!"

Ball's eyes narrowed. "He came around to see me, kid. I think you oughta know that he claims he isn't Joe Seltzer." His grin was crooked. "Claims he was an Army scout up to a couple of months ago. Showed me an Army discharge to back it up. He convinced yore sister. She took him to meet yore folks."

Jeff's jaws corded. "Army scout? How'd he get to know about the money hidden out here, then?"

Ball shrugged. "He didn't say. But he claims there were three maps. Cory Bates had one. He had one. And a man named Oley Jones had the third. They were the three survivors of the hold-up. They buried the money out in the Soapstones somewhere, and each man made out a portion of the map to the cache. Takes all three maps to find it, or nobody finds it!" Ball shook his head. "That's what he told us, Jeff. But you say you got hold of only one map—the one this Army scout had?"

Jeff nodded. "I told you. Bates didn't have anything on him except some change. Somebody got his map, then—the man who killed him." He

101

frowned. "This Oley Jones, maybe?"

"Jones hasn't shown up yet," Ball muttered.

Jeff started to pace. "The blazes with it! I've got one part of the map, anyway. And as long as I have it, no one else is going to pick up that money!"

"Reckon that's the way it is," Ball agreed. He tossed the gunny sack down by the fire. "Brought you some grub. Stay clear of town for a while. I'll tell yore folks something to ease their worry."

He started to turn his mule around. His tone lowered. "Maybe next time I come up here, I'll be bringing company." His lips pulled hard against his teeth. "That Army scout—"

Jeff nodded, his eyes bright. "I'll be waiting for him," he muttered. His hand slid down over his Colt butt. "Nobody's going to get that money, Ball—nobody except me!"

— VII —

— TANGLED LIVES —

THE STEELE horse ranch lay southeast of Bitter Wells, on a windy bench with the mass of Tortilla Butte blotting out the southern sky. From its wide veranda, a man could see a long way across the broken country to the uplands of New Mexico. Behind the butte, across the burning, lava-studded sink called the Soapstone badlands, a man could make Mexico in less than two days. . . .

The spread was small, but showed evidence of planning and a love of horses. A wind pump sucked water out of the desolate land and deposited it into a cement-lined tank where several horses stood like silhouettes against the night sky.

Miriam told Wes some of the background of the horse ranch as they rode through the star-studded night.

"Dad always loved horses," she said. "I think I inherit that love. When we came here, Mother wanted to settle in town. But Dad thought it would be too obvious. A cranky old man named Abe Jenkins owned this place . . . or rather the tumbledown shack and rickety corral that were here before. He wanted to sell out, and we bought this place for five hundred dollars. That was about all the money we had.

"Jenkins was trapping wild horses for a living. He told us about the bands roaming the hills south of here, and Jeff and Dad went after them. Most of the horses they caught were pretty poor specimens. But once in a while they brought in some really magnificent animals. They sold a few horses to an Army remount buyer and picked up a contract to supply Fort Milton. We don't entirely depend on what we trap, of course—Dad raises horses now, and we buy some, too. Mr. Havens, who owns the Crosshatch cattle ranch, sees us every fall about animals for his remuda, too."

Wes listened quietly. It was a long time since he had talked with a woman. For most of his life he had been a restless and unsettled man, and women had played a small part in it.

The girl looked at him, a little troubled. His silence bothered her.

She had accepted him at face value back in Ball's Stables, almost with relief. He was big and capable, and he had said he was not one of Dave Bettes' men, nor was he Joe Seltzer.

But was he her father's friend?

She pulled aside on a small knoll to give her mare a breather. The lights of Bitter Wells were lost behind them. Low hills hid her father's ranch ahead. Over them blazed a million brilliant stars.

Wes looked at her, sensing her thoughts.

"This isn't a woman's country," he said bluntly. "Nor what you did usually a woman's job." He let a brief silence hang between them; then: "Why didn't your father come looking for Jeff?"

"He was hurt last week, trying to stop raiders from running off some of our horses. They rode him down—"

She looked off into the distance. The night was soft, warm and dry. "Someone has to look

105

after Jeff," she whispered.

He nodded absently, thinking of the tough kid he had met in Ball's stables . . . the boy with the peppermint breath. His eyes hardened. Fifty thousand dollars was a lot of money. Did he have a right to it?

Miriam broke into his thoughts. "How did you know about the money buried here?"

Wes took a moment before answering. Her shield of mannishness was gone, and in the darkness he sensed her softness and her troubled doubts.

"I ran into Joe Seltzer five hundred miles east of here," he said. "I tried to save his life—"

He told her the rest of the story, without sparing himself.

"I came after Joe's share of the money. I was planning to go into Mexico with it, perhaps South America." He paused, then added levelly, "It's more money than I'll probably ever have in my lifetime."

"And now?" she questioned bitterly.

He shrugged. "I don't know." He looked off into a rising wind. "I think we'd better be getting on."

THEY RODE in silence after that, and Wes left her alone with her thoughts.

They came to the Steele ranch after ten. A lone light showed in the kitchen window. Darkness hid the rest of the spread.

The door opened as they rode into the yard, and a dim light splashed out across the veranda and down the steps, spraying against the feet of their horses. A man moved into the doorway, limping, his shadow blotting out most of the light. The rifle swung sharply around toward them.

"Dad!" Miriam said quickly. "It's me!"

The man shuffled out to the porch, easing away from the lighted doorway, merging with the darkness from the overhang. He propped the rifle, muzzle up, against the wall and turned to them, his voice weary.

"Where's Jeff, Miriam?"

Miriam's answer was slow in coming. "I don't know. Still looking for our horses, I imagine."

"Not Jeff!" the older man said bitterly. "He's not that crazy about horses!" Then he came to the edge of the veranda and looked Wes over, his expression hidden by the darkness.

107

"Who's he?"

"Wes Martin," Miriam replied. She slid out of the saddle. "He's come for a share of the Wells Fargo money."

Brandon Steele stiffened. "You, too?" He came around to the head of the stairs, and now the starlight revealed him to Wes. There were bags under Brandon's eyes and deep furrows in his sun-blackened, weathered face. He wore a straight gray mustache under a thin beak of a nose, and his mouth was a tight, thin line. A hard man on the long side of forty, perhaps—he looked even older, and Wes remembered his three years at Yuma.

"Come in," Brandon invited him shortly, and limped back inside the house.

A FRAIL-LOOKING, stoop-shouldered woman with iron-gray hair pulled back in a tight, severe bun on the nape of her thin neck stood in the big living room, furnished with several pieces of horsehair furniture. Several Navajo blankets pinned to the walls added to the brightness of the room. Straw mats were laid over the wide board floor.

108

She stood by the small table where a tintype of the family, possibly eleven or twelve years old, was mounted in an oval frame. Brandon Steele and the woman stood in a stiff pose, while two youngsters in starched clothes stared wide-eyed into the camera lens.

She was an angular, harsh-mouthed woman now, but in the picture she had a softness and a hint of sweetness, and her posture was straight. Watching her, Wes could see the changes Brandon's three years in Yuma Penitentiary had wrought in her.

She came over to Miriam, her voice harsh and unfriendly. "Where's Jeff?" She ignored Wes altogether. "Where is he, Miriam?"

The girl seemed to shrink from her mother, as from an uplifted hand. "I didn't find him. But Mr. Hotchkiss said that Jeff had been in town, looking for the men who stole our horses—"

"Horses!" Contempt rang in her mother's voice. "Horses! Will horses ever pay for the misery I've suffered? For the shame?" She shook her finger under Miriam's nose, self-pity making her voice shrill. "No! Jeff isn't out looking for horses—for your precious mare! He's after our

109

money, Miriam—you hear?" She whirled on Wes. "I heard Miriam say you were after the money, too! But you can't have it!" She was close to bitter tears now. "That money is rightfully ours! We paid for it in tears and shame—"

"Mother—" Miriam said, her cheeks flaming.

The woman whirled on her. "It's ours!" she repeated angrily. "And no one else is entitled to it."

"Mary, Mary," Brandon interrupted her softly. He put his arm around her, but she stiffened and drew away from him. Brandon sighed. He looked at his daughter, who was standing rigid, hurt by her mother's disregard, her lack of restraint.

"Take Mister Martin to the kitchen, Miriam," Brandon said. "Perhaps he'd like a cup of coffee." His voice sharpened slightly as Miriam made no move. "Go ahead. I want a word with your mother."

Miriam turned and made a motion toward the kitchen. Her voice was small as she looked at Wes. "Please . . ." she said softly.

"I want my son!" Mary Steele cried. "I want Jeff, you hear! He's my boy! He knows what I've

110

been through, how I've suffered!"

Brandon took hold of her arm firmly. "I know," he said grimly. "We'll talk about Jeff—in private."

Wes watched him lead his bitter wife toward the bedroom. Then he became aware of Miriam's anguished gaze.

"I'm sorry," he said quietly. "I didn't know—"

She turned to the kitchen, and he followed her, feeling like a man who had inadvertently pried into something he shouldn't have.

The kitchen was neat and clean, and a woman's touch was evident in the curtains at the window and the small vase of straw flowers in the center of the kitchen table.

Wes paused, feeling grimy and unkempt in that room. The gun weighing against his thigh made him uncomfortable.

She looked at him, sensing his uneasiness, and Wes smiled wryly. "Guess I've eaten out so much I've forgotten what a woman's kitchen is like." He made a gesture toward the sink. "Mind if I wash?"

Miriam came up and took his hat and hung it on a peg while Wes washed at the kitchen sink

111

and dried his face and hands on the towel she provided.

When he was clean, he sat at the round table, and Miriam poured coffee. She took a cup for herself and joined him; she looked less boyish in the lamplight with her hair loosened over her shoulders.

"Mother's never forgotten those years," she said sadly. Her smile was tremulous. She was hurt. Her mother had chosen to disregard her daughter in front of a stranger, had made her seem unwanted and guilty. And though she tried to hide it behind her smile and her words, Wes sensed the deep pain in her.

"I hate that money!" she said with a sudden burst of feeling. "It's ruined our lives. We used to be a happy family. But when Dad was sent to prison, Mother changed. And she changed Jeff, too."

Outside, the wind had picked up, and grit tapped against the kitchen windows. There seemed to be more in the night than the sound of grit—there was a far off wailing sound in the wind, like a woman lost in bottomless grief.

Wes could think of nothing to say to her. He

112

thought of the money he had come for, money buried somewhere out in that desolate wasteland; of how that money seemed to have trapped many people.

Two men had died taking it—Voss Grant and Rocky Callahan. Joe Seltzer was dead, too, and so was Cory Bates. And for all he knew, Oley Jones was, also. All of them were tied in one way or another to that money.

And the Steeles—the stolen money had trapped them, too.

"Dad brought us here because of Mother and Jeff," Miriam went on. She sat stiffly, looking down into her cup, ashamed to let Wes see the hurt in her eyes again. "He came here because of the money. But he changed his mind." She looked up at him now, her eyes intent. "He's forgotten those terrible years at Yuma. He and I have come to like it here. It's clean and bright, and no one knows us. We have our horses, and they make us a good living." She looked toward the door, and sadness crept into her voice again. "If only Jeff and Mother could see that what we have here is more than money—"

Wes finished his coffee and stood up. Miriam

113

kept her eyes on her cup. "I've talked too much," she said slowly, "haven't I?"

"It's late," Wes replied.

She stood up and faced him. "I'm sure Father wants to talk to you—"

Wes shrugged. "Some other time." He crossed to his hat and took it down; he was conscious of her eyes on him.

"I gave you the wrong impression this afternoon, didn't I?" Her voice was low.

He turned and faced her and shook his head.

"I didn't thank you for trying to help this afternoon. I should have. But I was worried about Jeff—"

"So am I," Brandon said. He came into the kitchen, looking tired and discouraged. He looked at Wes and frowned. "You leaving?"

Wes nodded.

Brandon looked at his daughter. "You said he was after that money?" His gaze swung back to Wes. "You one of them? Or are you a Wells Fargo agent?"

"Neither one," Wes answered.

Brandon studied him coldly. "Then how do you know about the money?"

114

"Joe Seltzer told him," Miriam said. She came to stand near her father. "He was an Army scout when he met Seltzer. Seltzer was dying. He told Wes about the money—"

"Let him tell it, Miriam!" Brandon's voice was thin.

"That's about the way it was," Wes said. "Joe had an Apache arrow in him. He told me about the money, and he gave me his portion of a map to where the money was buried."

Brandon took a deep breath. "A map?" His eyes turned bitter, and he sat down at the table. "So the money is buried out here somewhere?"

Wes frowned. "Didn't you know?"

"Not for sure," Brandon replied. "We guessed—" His voice turned flat. "That is, my wife and Jeff did." He looked up at Wes. "So you want Joe Seltzer's share?"

"That's what I came for," Wes said. He looked at Miriam. "I'm not sure now."

"Why not?" Brandon's lips twisted bitterly. "One hundred and fifty thousand dollars—"

"Is a lot of money," Wes agreed. He was thinking of the assailant with the peppermint odor on his breath, who had clubbed him uncon-

115

scious in Cory Bates' room.

"It could make a lot of difference to this spread of yours," he added.

"I'm out on parole," Brandon said stiffly. He glanced toward the door. The hard lines of his lips had been fashioned by his years at Yuma, and they didn't smile—but his eyes did, in a sad sort of way.

"That first year in prison I hated everyone. I could have killed the prosecutor who built up the circumstantial evidence that convinced the jury I was in with those holdup men. I could have killed the judge who sentenced me, and the jurors who found me guilty.

"By the end of three years I still hated everyone, but not in the same way. All I really wanted by then was to get out. Well, I got out on parole. I found my son almost grown and my daughter a young woman. In addition, my wife had changed."

He was silent for a moment, bitter and retrospective. "She never got over my being sent to prison. She had moved from where we lived, and she and Jeff had kept track of every news story printed about the holdup. It narrowed things

116

down to Bitter Wells—to the Soapstone badlands. Their trail had vanished beyond this point. So we made a guess that the holdup men must have buried the money somewhere and split up. We had no way of knowing if they had already returned and picked it up. After all, it was more than three years later when we got here. But Mary and Jeff insisted that we come. Mary had a stubborn conviction that the money was buried somewhere around Bitter Wells, and that the thieves would come back some day, and we'd know them. She feels, blindly perhaps, that the money is rightfully ours now—"

"And you?" Wes asked the question levelly.

Brandon shrugged. "I don't want the money. All I want is to live in peace here. I've always liked horses. I like to raise them. Here we've had luck trapping some pretty fine mustangs. Once in a while we catch one like that strawberry roan of Miriam's—Fantasy."

"Fantasy?" Wes' tone held amusement.

Miriam colored. "My name for her." Her lips tightened. "She was stolen a few days ago."

"You've been having trouble with horse thieves?"

"Not often." Brandon made a tired gesture. "But once in a while Bettes' boys get anxious for new mounts. They're a hard, clanny bunch—" He paused and eyed Wes. "You've met Dave Bettes?"

Wes nodded.

"I have a hunch most of his men are wanted by the law. They use his place on Dry Creek as a hideout. Bill Havens over at Crosshatch has been losing beef, and he's getting riled. But so far he hasn't been prodded into doing anything. And the sheriff is too far away to give much protection." He shook his head.

"Unofficially, Dave Bettes runs Bitter Wells. He's a self-appointed justice of the peace, whatever that means, and he's appointed that gunslinger, Vic Arness, as his special deputy. I don't know how he managed it, but he has the sanction of the sheriff's office. Probably it's because this country is too big and wild for Sheriff Ventley, and he's glad to have someone represent the law here. About all Dave and Vic do is collect taxes, or throw some drunken puncher in jail after a night in town and fine him in the morning."

Wes frowned, his thoughts working on an

118

angle which had just occurred to him. "This man Bettes—how long has he been in Bitter Wells?"

Brandon shrugged.

"He was here when we came—not quite two years ago. Don't know how long he had been here before that. Why?"

"A hunch," Wes answered. He looked at Miriam, then past her to the dark window facing the yard.

What had seemed like a simple matter of collecting Joe Seltzer's share of stolen money had turned into an involved affair which clouded his own motives. He had been willing to take that one step outside the law for fifty thousand dollars, but he knew now that that one step would have been only the beginning.

Like Brandon's son, Jeff, he reflected. The boy wanted the money out of a warped sense of the injustice done to his father. But for Jeff, too, it would be only the beginning of a dark and lonely road outside the law.

He still had time to clear out. But he felt sorry for this bitter man—and for Miriam.

"You were right about the money being buried in the Soapstones," he told Brandon.

119

"But this is how they worked it."

He explained about the maps. "Cory Bates showed up in town first and was killed. Whoever killed him was after the map he had on him. When I went up to his room I was slugged." He meet Brandon's gaze evenly. "It was your son who ambushed me, Brandon. He was in that room, with Bates' body—"

Brandon recoiled as though he had been struck across the face. "No—" he whispered. "Jeff couldn't—"

He glanced at Miriam, seeking her reassurance.

Miriam's face was white. "Jeff! You can't be sure, Wes."

"Unless there's someone else who likes peppermints," Wes said grimly.

Brandon groaned. "He's wild. I know that. And I know how much he wants that money. But to kill a man—"

"I don't think *he* killed Bates," Wes said. "But he was there when I walked in—and I think he's got the map Joe Seltzer had given me."

Brandon's voice was thick, helpless. "So help me, mister—I don't want that money! And when

120

I see Jeff—" His voice choked off.

Wes said: "I thought I'd better tell you. He can have the map, as far as I'm concerned." He smiled thinly at Brandon's quick regard.

"I knew it was stolen money when I came here. I tried to fool myself into making excuses that I had earned it by trying to save Joe Seltzer's life. But that money belongs to Wells Fargo—not to me or Oley Jones—or your son Jeff."

Brandon's voice was a thin whisper. "I know."

Miriam said: "Then you're not staying in Bitter Wells?"

Wes shook his head. "Thanks for getting me out of jail." He turned to Brandon. "And thank you for setting me straight about that money—"

"Stay!" Brandon said, cutting in thickly. He stood up and crossed to Wes. "Help me."

"How?"

"Get that money off my mind, and I'll be thankful to you for the rest of my days!"

Wes was silent.

"I'm thinking of my son," Brandon said. "Get that money before he does—turn it back to Wells Fargo. Just get it before Jeff goes too far. . . ."

He looked at his daughter. "I'm too crippled

121

to do much riding—and I don't want Miss Miriam to go back to that town." He paused, swung back to Wes.

"I don't know you, mister. But I need you. And I have to trust someone" His voice sank, low and bitter. "I have to trust someone," he repeated.

Wes hesitated.

He had been willing to gamble his life for fifty thousand dollars. Now he was being asked to risk it for the sake of a wild kid he didn't know.

He started to shake his head.

Miriam said: "Please, Wes. I trust you."

He looked at her. It was a woman he was looking at, not a tomboy. In the lamplight she looked older than her years, softer. . . .

He took a deep breath. Maybe there was something here more valuable than fifty thousand dollars.

"I'll try," he said. "I guess I owe you that much." He turned to Brandon. "I came to town as Joe Seltzer. Only you and Ball Hotchkiss know I'm not Joe. I'll have to keep on being Seltzer, but I'll need your help—and Hotchkiss will have to help, too."

122

"He will!" Miriam said quickly. "He's been our friend since we came to Bitter Wells. He's the only one who knows about Father's connection with the stolen money."

Brandon held out his hand. "I'd ask you to stay the night. But there's only Jeff's room, and Mary would—"

"I understand," Wes said.

They went with him to the porch. Wes mounted his stallion. The animal whinnied softly.

"That's some horse you're riding," Brandon observed. He came down the steps and ran a palm appreciatively over the roan's nose.

"He's all I own," Wes said. He looked at Miriam. "I'll keep an eye out for your horse, Fantasy."

She nodded wordlessly. Wes swung away from the veranda, and they watched him merge into the night.

Miriam said: "Good night, Wes," and Brandon turned sharply and watched her. She stiffened under his scrutiny. He sighed.

"We're asking him to risk his life," Brandon said. "Have we the right?"

Miriam didn't answer. Her eyes were on the dark shape on the road. . . . She shivered slightly. "Maybe I have," she whispered.

— VIII —

— BIG MACK —

IT WAS A FEW minutes after eleven when Wes returned to Bitter Wells. The wind was in his face all the way, dry and gritty. It was an unseen brittle thing, pushing against him, wailing overhead.

He was glad to see the town ahead of him—a dark scattering of buildings with only a light or two probing the murky darkness. Evidently Bitter Wells retired early, he thought. There was little to do in a town like this after dark. What night life there was probably took place in the saloon, and he was not particularly surprised, therefore, to see that the Aces High Saloon lights were still on.

He turned into Ball's stable yard and dismounted. There was no light burning in Ball's living quarters, which were tacked onto the northern end of the frame structure. But there was a dim light shining inside the barn. Wes led his mount up the ramp; inside, he unsaddled the roan and turned him into an empty stall. He gave the stallion a quick rubdown, forked some hay into the bin and measured out a half-bucket of oats from an open feed sack. He heard Miriam's terrier, Prince, snort at him from the darkness at the far end of the barn, and he grinned.

He found a bucket and went out into the yard and pumped water into it. The wind stung his face. He came back and put the bucket down for the roan, and in the net stall a big gray mule lifted his head above the side wall and snorted loudly.

Wes eyed the wrinkled lips and bared teeth. He walked over and patted the thick shaggy neck, and surprise narrowed his gaze. He reached over and ran his hand down the mule's side, finding the animal still warm and damp, and he knew that the mule had been ridden and only recently turned into the stall.

126

Then he heard a soft step behind him and turned to face Hotchkiss in underwear, pants and socks. The man had a shotgun cradled in his arms, and there was a harsh light in his eyes.

"Looking for something, mister?"

Wes shook his head. "Came back and didn't see a light in your room," he said. "Didn't want to disturb you, so I took care of my cayuse myself."

"Obliged," the stableman said. There was a faint edge of sarcasm in his tone. "But I'm a light sleeper, like I told you." He shuffled up, his left heel showing through a hole in his sock. He reached out and gently pushed the mule's muzzle and the animal whickered eagerly. "Go to sleep, Sampson," he growled, and turned to Wes. "Sampson don't look like much, but he kin outlast most horses in this kind of country."

"I believe you," Wes said shortly. Someone had ridden the mule tonight, but Ball evidently was not going to mention it. Wes shrugged. "Sorry I woke you up. See you in the morning."

The stableman asked: "You gonna stay in town?" He seemed greatly surprised.

"Why not?"

127

"Well— I thought, with Bettes having put you in jail and you having trouble with him—"

"I have a hunch Dave Bettes knows he made a mistake," Wes interrupted. "And I don't think his deputy will come after me again."

Ball eyed the big man facing him, a scowl on his face. "You seem pretty sure of yourself." He made a gesture toward the loft. "You're welcome to sleep here if you want."

Wes shook his head. "I'll try the hotel."

Ball's grin held a touch of admiration. "Might be you'll get a good night's sleep at that. But you're lucky that Dave's boys left town this afternoon."

"Dave's boys?"

"Yeah. Utah and Monte. But Big Mack's still in town. He's been drinking all day, and he gets mean instead of falling down drunk." He shrugged. "Thought I'd tell you, case you run into him on your way to the hotel."

"Thanks." Wes' voice was dry.

"Jeff tangled with him earlier today. You saw what the kid looked like." Ball made a gesture. "He came to town looking for his sister's horse. So he told me. Found it tied up in front of the saloon—a strawberry roan mare with four white stockings. Big Mack claimed it was his cayuse; Jeff swore the mare was one of those stolen from his father's horse spread."

"Could be," Wes murmured.

"I didn't see the animal," Ball muttered. "And from what Jeff told me, they hadn't put a brand on the mare. Something about his sister not being able to stand a hot iron against the mare's flank. Anyway, if it came right down to it, it would be Miriam Steele's word against Big Mack's."

"I see," Wes replied. "And a lady's word doesn't count for much in Bitter Wells?"

Ball scowled. "Only thing that counts in this town is a fast gun."

Wes eyed the sloppy man for an instant. The stableowner seemed genuinely concerned about the Steeles. But how far could *he* trust the man?

"I had a talk with Brandon Steele," he said levelly. "He's worried about his son. I told him I'd try to help." He glanced toward the loft. "Jeff come back?"

Ball shook his head. "But he will. I'll send him home."

"See that he does," Wes said. "I wouldn't want him to get in my way."

He started to leave, but stopped in the doorway. "I told Brandon who I was. But it would be better if I remained Joe Seltzer in town. Brandon agreed." He eyed Ball. "He said you would, too."

Ball made a quick gesture. "Of course."

He watched Wes step out into the yard. He didn't move. After Wes' footsteps had faded away, he moved back to the stall and ran his hand over Sampson's flank.

"I wonder," he mused. His eyes held a cold and deadly light.

THE WIND had a sullen sound in town. Out on the flats, it had moaned like a woman in distress. Here it had an angry mutter, like a man searching for the lover who had run off with his wife.

Wes' boots clumped hollowly on the gang walk. He was coming up to the saloon when the windows of the Aces High went dark. He paused, a tall man in the shadows, suddenly alert.

There was an alleyway between him and the

saloon—a passageway for wagons bringing supplies to the saloon store shed. Probably it led to a
loading platform in back.

In the shrouding blackness of the alley, a
horse neighed in anger and fright, and a man's
thick, slightly blurred voice rang out.

"Come on, you red bitch! Hold still, or I'll
break yore blasted back!"

There was a flurry of movement, the thudding
of a man's first against the horse's ribs. Wes
came to his toes, his eyes narrowing coldly.

There was movement in the shadows at the
mouth of the alley. Then a large man came out
into the starshine of the street, pulling hard on
the bridle of a horse. He was holding the animal
by the bit iron, and he was powerful enough to
hold the mare down, keeping it from rearing and
striking out at him. He had his right hand
clenched, and his fist thumped against the mare's
ribs again.

Wes could see that the horse had four white
stockings. It was too dark to make out what color
it was, but he had a hunch this was Miriam's
horse, Fantasy.

Even as he watched, the mare jerked sharply

131

and broke Big Mack's grip. She reared then and struck at him with flying front hoofs, and the big man barely evaded them. He lurched aside, and the mare whirled and went pounding away from him, down the street.

"Come back, you ——!" Big Mack's swearing took a deadly turn. He drew his Colt and was aiming at the fleeing animal when Wes' quick shot tore the gun from his hand.

The shot seemed to ricochet through town, whipped by the desert wind. The big man turned quickly, like some startled grizzily. He saw Wes move out to the edge of the boardwalk and stared at him, realization coming slowly across his broad, brutish features.

"That's no way to treat a horse," Wes said coldly, "especially a horse you don't own!"

Big Mack started to move toward the Army scout. He stood a few inches taller, he was thicker through the waist and chest, and his arms were like wagon tongues. He looked like a man who could bend a horseshoe between his hands— and had!

"You meddling fool!" he snarled. "I'm gonna take that gun away from you an' jam it down yore throat!"

"You'd better sleep it off, fella!" Wes advised him bleakly.

"The name's Big Mack!" the man sneered. "And I'm gonna beat the living daylights out of you!"

"I think your mouth's bigger than you are!" Wes snapped. He thrust his gun back into his holster and stepped off the walk to meet the man.

Big Mack lunged forward, bringing his balled right fist around in a vicious roundhouse swing for Wes' face. The Army scout ducked and buried his fist in Big Mack's stomach, elbowed him under the chin with the same hand in a quick upward jolt and pivoted around with an open-handed slap to the man's face.

It was a contemptuous handling of the bully, and it shook Big Mack's confidence more than it hurt him. He stood braced on wide-spread feet, his face stinging, his head buzzing slightly. He had bitten his lips, and blood trickled down his chin. He wiped it away.

"A fancy Dan, eh?" he growled. "Just for that I'll break you in two!"

Wes' gunshot seemed to have aroused no one

133

—or if it had, no one bothered to investigate. There were only the two of them in the street in front of the darkened saloon, and the sullen wind swirling dust. . . .

Wes said harshly, "If you had any sense you'd quit now and go sleep it off!"

Big Mack lunged for him again. He was more cunning this time. He tried to grapple with Wes Martin, get hold of him so that he could bring his greater might and weight into play.

Wes sidestepped, felt Big Mack's fingers claw at his shirt and struck down sharply with the edge of his palm on the other's forearm. Big Mack grunted with pain and drew his hand back, and Wes stepped in and belted him a quick one-two in the mouth. He stepped away before Big Mack's outreaching hands could close on him. The man stumbled, and Wes came in again, driving his blows, getting the solid pivot of his wide shoulders behind them.

Big Mack's wheezy grunts were audible above the wind. He was spun around, and his knees got rubbery. But a stubborn rage held him up. He pawed at Wes like a tormented bear, and Wes hammered at him, wanting it to end now.

Big Mack's nose broke under the impact of one of Wes' punches. Blood spilled down his face and dripped over his shirt and was sucked up by the dry earth under his feet. He wiped at his face with the back of his sleeve and tried to find the shadowy figure who moved like a cat and struck with the kick of a mule.

Wes finally caught him with a solid smash under the left ear. Big Mack stumbled, and his hands dropped, and Wes belted him on the side of his jaw. Big Mack turned all the way around and fell across the walk, his face banging on the boards.

Wes brushed hair from his eyes and sucked in gulps of air. The big man had taken a lot of punishment, but Wes remembered Jeff Steele's face and the way the man had treated Miriam's mare, and he had no regrets. He found his hat, which had been knocked off during the fight, and set it on his head. Then he walked to the unconscious man, not wanting to leave him lying there. He was bending over Big Mack when he heard a man clear his throat cautiously. Wes whirled, his Colt appearing as by magic in his hand.

The man in the saloon doorway was a thin

135

shape—who shrank away from Wes' leveled gun.

Wes snapped: "Come out where I can get a good look at you!"

The figure moved out to the edge of the walk. He was a thin, balding man, still wearing a bartender's wet apron. He had his hands clasped across the top of his head, indicating his pacifist inclinations.

Wes relaxed slightly. "Friend of yours?"

The bartender shrugged. "Big Mack drinks here. He's one of Dave Bettes' riders." He added softly: "Dave owns this saloon. I only work for him."

Wes nodded. "Case you didn't see it, I'm telling you how it happened. He was maltreating a horse that didn't belong to him. I stopped him." Martin walked over to where Big Mack's Colt lay in the street dust. He picked it up, ejected the rounds, thrust them into his pocket and came back to hand the gun to the bartender.

"Give it to him later. If he still wants to take this up in the morning, tell him I'll be in town all day."

He moved away, heading for the Mesa House looming up darkly across the street.

136

ZEKE EMONS, the bartender, waited until the big man stirred. Big Mack groaned and pawed at the boards and finally flopped over on his back. The bartender made no move to help him. He had no love for Big Mack.

He heard someone move in the dark empty sawdust floored room behind him and turned; he was not too surprised when Dave Bettes loomed up. The man didn't look any cleaner in night clothes. He had on long underwear and socks and a flat-crowned hat, and his left cheek bulged under a wad of tobacco.

Emons wondered with sour interest if Dave Bettes slept with that chaw and that hat—he had never seen his boss without either.

He could smell Bettes even at the distance separating them, but he kept from showing his displeasure. The man had a nasty disposition at any time.

"Thought I heard a shot," Bettes growled. He looked down at Big Mack; then, muttering with stark amazement, he bent over his rider. "Blazes! It's Big Mack!" He looked up at his bartender. "What happened?"

"Ran into somebody he couldn't lick, looks

137

like," Emons muttered. He stiffened at the anger he saw on Bettes' face. "Heck, I was closing up, Dave. Finally got Big Mack to leave. He went out through the back door for that mare he had stashed in the shed, and I put out the lights and was coming upstairs when I heard a shot." He shrugged. "I came out in time to see this fella, a stranger, whip the blazes out of Big Mack."

"Stranger? A big fella?"

"Well, not as big as Mack, but big enough." Emons described Wes. "Don't really know what happened. I could hear Big Mack having trouble with that red mare. Then there was a shot. When I got out here, the mare was gone and Big Mack was getting a licking—"

Big Mack's voice was thick with swallowed blood. "I'll kill the son—" He was getting up, a shambling, wobbly man. He staggered and fell against the side of the saloon and braced himself, pawing at the blood on his face. "I'll kill him—" But there was no conviction in his shaky voice.

"You darn fool!" Bettes snarled. "I told you to get back to the ranch with Utah. If you had listened to me—"

"I do what I want!" Big Mack mumbled. He

138

reached for his Colt in a blind surge of anger and fumbled at his empty holster for several seconds before he realized he was weaponless.

Bettes took hold of his anger. He couldn't push the big man too far, he knew, as he knew he couldn't push the others he hired. But he might be able to use him. . . .

"Help him up to Vic's room," he told his bartender. "He can stay there for the night." He heard Emons' thin question, and he snapped back: "Vic's gone out of town. That nester's wife—" Then he turned back to Big Mack, who was protesting thickly.

"Shut up!" he told the battered man. "You're in no shape to ride. Looks like you met the Santa Fe Express head on. Get upstairs with Zeke. Do what I say, and you might get a chance to get even with that fella who handed you this beating."

Big Mack pushed away from the wall. "Sand in my eyes," he mumbled. "Couldn't see him. Next time I'll—"

"Yeah, yeah—next time," Dave said coldly. He waited until Big Mack stumbled off into the darkness of the saloon behind Zeke. He stood scowling, an incongruous figure in his long johns and black hat, peering across the murky street.

"Mebbe you're just a tough hombre on the run, fella," he muttered. "And mebbe you're something else. We'll find out in the morning."

He wanted to talk to Vic Arness. But his deputy had ridden out of town right away after they had jailed the man who called himself Joe Seltzer. Dave knew where Vic had gone—where he went periodically, tipped off by some arrangement only he seemed to know. There was a nester's wife down along one of the Sweetwater's feeders whose husband sometimes had to go to Caldwell for an overnight stay.

"Blast these young goats," he muttered. "He'll walk into a load of buckshot one fine night," he prophesied grimly.

He went back inside the saloon, closing and barring the door. He crossed the empty room, still reeking with the smell of sour beer and stale tobacco and opened the small door leading to the store shed in back.

A figure stirred in the darkness, and a cot creaked.

Bettes called: "Jim!"

140

"Yeah?" There was a trace of temper in the sleepy voice. Bettes pictured the lanky, white-haired bum who swamped out of his saloon, and his voice hardened. "I want you to ride out to the ranch tonight. I want you to get Utah and Monte back to town. You tell them I want them in Bitter Wells by noon."

Jim muttered rebelliously.

"They better be here, Jim!" Bettes said viciously, and slammed the door shut behind him.

As he headed upstairs, he knew Jim would do as he had been told.

— IX —

— THE LETTER —

WES MARTIN awakened as the sun was slanting lazily through his windows. It turned the flimsy curtains into shabby strips of cloth which fluttered like some dismal trapped thing against the sill.

The wind still blew outside the window, and sand had sifted across the floor in a thin coating of gray dust. Wes' lips felt dry. He rolled over and stood up and stretched. He had slept with the door locked and his gun close at hand—and he was a light sleeper.

He had been given a room closer to the head of the stairs, overlooking the street—a room, the desk clerk had explained hurriedly, which had just been vacated that evening. Wes knew the man had lied. The staleness of the cubicle was of long standing.

As he dressed, Wes looked into the streaked mirror, seeing a face that looked gaunt and drawn behind a three-day stubble. He had left his warbag in Dave Bettes' office, and his shaving gear was in it. He thought of this, and the vague plan that had formed in his mind during the ride back to town from the Steele horse ranch seemed suddenly clearer now, as though his mind had kept on working on it during the night.

More than ever he was convinced that Jeff had not killed Cory Bates; that it had been Oley Jones who had shot Cory. Oley Jones was in Bitter Wells, hiding behind the innocent façade of one of Bitter Wells' citizens. It had to be that way. Oley Jones, a stranger, could not have come to the desert town without being instantly noticed, as he and Cory Bates had been. But Cory Jones, living in town under another name and identity, could easily have slipped up the Mesa House's back stairs and waited in Cory's room— as he had intended, no doubt, to wait for Joe Seltzer when Joe showed up.

Dave Bettes? The man fitted the loose description Seltzer had given Wes, allowing for the passage of five years. It could be Bettes, but Wes

143

had to make sure.

He came down into the dingy lobby with its dusty potted palms and brass cuspidors and saw that Kenny, the desk clerk, was talking to a shaggy-haired oldster who kept shaking his head with mulish insistence.

"Can't take it back. No return address on it." The old man's voice sounded peevish. "When did this feller Bates die?"

Wes turned to the desk. Kenny lookeed up at him and frowned.

"Something for my friend Cory Bates?" Wes asked pleasantly.

The old man turned to look at him. "You know him?"

"I was his friend."

"I'm Pop Willis," the oldster grumbled. "Run the feed store down the block. I generally get over to Caldwell once a week for feed, and I pick up the mail for Bitter Wells—what there is of it. Got a letter for a Cory Bates, addressed to him at the Mesa House. But Kenny tells me that Bates is dead?"

"That's right," Wes said. He held out his hand. I'll take the letter for him."

144

"Whoa!" Pop said, backing away and putting his hand with the letter behind his back. "Wait a minute, young feller. I got no right to hand you a piece of United States mail that ain't addressed to you."

"Is there a return address on it?"

"Wal—" Pop hesitated. "No, there ain't. But—"

"In that case, you can't return it, can you?" Wes pressed. "That means the letter remains there, as part of Mr. Bates' personal property. And as I'm his only living friend and relative, that makes me his heir." Wes' tone was firm, as though this were indisputable. "Therefore, I am legally entitled to examine and dispose of all and any of Mister Cory Bates' personal and worldly goods."

Pop picked at his scraggly beard in confusion. "Wal—I don't know—" He turned to Kenny for support. The desk clerk was staring in open-mouthed wonder at Wes.

"This jasper telling the truth, Kenny?" Pop's voice indicated that Kenny's testimony would be of paramount importance. "He a friend of this Bates feller?"

145

Kenny nodded weakly. "He said he was—"

Wes took the letter from Pop. "I'll give you a receipt for it, Mr. Willis," he said crisply. He turned to Kenny. "A piece of notepaper, if you please."

Kenny obeyed. Wes used the register pen and scribbled out a receipt, heading it: *"To Whom It May Concern."*

Pop took it and scratched his head. "Reckon it's all right," he mumbled. He walked away, shaking his head.

"By the way," Wes turned to Kenny, "where is my deceased friend, Mr. Bates?"

"On a slab in Gus Myers' shed. Gus is the local carpenter—he's going to make a box for him. I understand he'll be buried in Boot Hill this afternoon."

Wes placed a double eagle on the counter. "See that he gets a decent burial."

Outside, he eased his hard frame against one of the supports in front of the hotel and looked up and down the street. Pop Willis was just turning into his feed store. A couple of men were heading for the Chinese restaurant. He turned and walked up the street to Dave Bettes' office,

146

but found it closed. There was no sign of life in the saloon at that hour of the morning.

Wes headed for the red and white painted barber pole a few doors to the south. A small brown man with thick black hair growing like a bush on his head was sweeping off the walk.

Wes said: "You open?" and Tony nodded.

"First customer every Friday I give a massage of the face. For free." Tony beamed. "You are the first, *señor*. I give you a good massage, no?"

"Yes," Wes grinned. He walked inside the small shop and sat down in the one chair, and while Tony busied himself he took out the letter addressed to Bates and tore it open.

A ragged, worn piece of wrapping paper was the only thing enclosed; a piece of paper similar to the one Joe Seltzer had given Wes—a map. There was nothing else; no explanation, no additional information.

Wes frowned, trying to puzzle it out. Tony was babbling about the lack of newcomers to Bitter Wells, the possibility of a railroad spur, the hot winds which periodically plagued the town.

But Wes Martin's thoughts were centered on the map in his hands. Why had Cory Bates

147

mailed himself a copy of his portion of the map? Or was it a copy? Was this really the original map Bates had drawn and, not trusting his fellow thieves, had mailed to himself as insurance against his untimely death?

It could be. In that case the man who had killed Bates had come away empty-handed.

Something else occurred to Wes now; something that made him sit up abruptly. Tony stepped back, clicking his scissors disapprovingly.

"*Diablo, señor!* How can I cut the hair—"

Wes settled back. "Sorry, Tony."

But he was thinking of young Jeff Steele. Whoever had killed Bates probably knew now that the Steele boy had taken Joe's map from him. If he had Cory's false map, and his own, then he would need only the map Jeff had taken from him to complete the set and find the money buried in the Soapstone badlands.

It could mean that young Steele was in deadly danger—or probably already dead!

His thoughts were interrupted by Tony. "Now for the massage, *señor*." The barber smiled, slapping a hot towel across Wes' face. . . .

148

— X —

— GUNFIGHT —

DAVE BETTES came out of his saloon and walked across the street to his office. He had seen Wes leave the Mesa House and enter the barbershop, and he walked slowly, ducking his head against the wind. It was not blowing hard, but it was persistent, and he knew it might last for several days.

Utah and Monte would be in a disagreeable mood when they showed up, and did not relish the unpleasant encounter.

He was unlocking his door when he saw Vic Arness ride by, hat pulled low over his eyes. He turned and yelled to the man, and the deputy turned and put his cayuse to the rack in front of the hotel. Dismounting, he stood for a moment, scowling at Dave.

"I need a cup of coffe," he said roughly.

"Later," Dave snapped. "Come inside." Vic looked as though he needed more than a cup of coffee. He looked a little worn around the edges, like a man who had slept little, and there was a long nail scratch under his chin.

Must be a regular hellcat, that nester woman, Dave thought. But his interest lagged. The hot tides of his youth had ebbed fast, and he saw little pleasure in the other sex now.

Vic followed him inside the office. There was a sullen look in the gunman's eyes.

"I ain't awake yet," he protested.

"This will wake you," Dave said coldly. "The big fella's back in town. The one who broke out of my jail last night."

Vic stiffened. "Thought he'd be clear into Mexico by now—"

"He's back in town." Dave's voice held a taunt. "Shows how much he thinks of you, Vic. He's in Tony's right now, getting himself a shave and a haircut."

Vic's eyes glinted angrily. "Don't see you

150

making any moves," he growled.

"Listen, you fool!" Dave snapped. "I pay you and the boys at the ranch to take care of things like this. You're the fast gun in town, Vic—not me. You're the mean, tough deputy paid to wear a badge. He's your job!"

Vic waited, his mouth turning dry.

"He came back," Dave went on, "to see how tough you really are. He came back last night, and Big Mack took him on. He gave Big Mack a licking."

Vic shook his head. "You're crazy!"

"Hah!" Dave walked around his desk and took a crooked cheroot from a tin box. "Ask Big Mack, if he can talk yet. He's up in your room. stretched out on your bed, with a busted nose and some cracked ribs."

Vic's hands went down in a nervous gesture over his Colt butt. He wiped the sweat from his palm on his pants.

"What do you want, Dave?"

"I want this hombre dead," Dave said bluntly.

Vic licked his lips. "From what you've been telling me, he's not going to be a pushover."

"Reckon he ain't," Dave replied. He was

151

scowling as he lighted his cigar. "He might be Joe Seltzer, Vic. Then again, he might be one of them range detectives Bill Havens over at Cross-hatch's been saying he's gonna send for."

Vic shook his head. "I don't like it."

"You don't have to like it!" Dave said. Then, reading the anger in Vic's eyes, he calmed down. "You don't have to brace him cold," he suggested. "Pull that old Tucson trick on him. I'll have a dozen witnesses who'll back you up in any inquiry. Don't forget," he went on swiftly, "I'm the law here in Bitter Wells. And you're my deppy." He saw hesitation flicker in Vic's eyes and he added: "There's an extra five hundred in it for you."

Greed made an appearance in Vic's eyes. He nodded. "You'll back me?"

"I said I would."

Vic licked his lips. "I'll be across the street. I need more than coffee for this job, Dave."

Bettes shrugged. "Don't take more than a bracer," he warned. He went to the door with his deputy and watched Vic cross the street and go into the saloon. Vic was a fast gun, and he was an old hand at the Tucson trick. He should not

have too much trouble taking care of this med-
dlesome stranger who had come to Bitter Wells.

WES MARTIN stepped out of Tony's barbershop with trouble far from his thoughts. He felt
clean and refreshed and in contrast Bitter Wells
looked dirtier and meaner than before to him as
he paused on the walk. The wind was blowing
against his broad back, prying with gritty fingers
at the nape of his neck. He took a deep breath
and thought of Miriam's brother, and wondered
if the boy had come back to Ball Hotchkiss'
stable.

Then he shrugged. He could stand a good
breakfast and a couple of cups of coffee first, he
thought. And with this in mind, he crossed the
street and turned south toward Ah Ling's restaurant.

The bartender he had talked with last night
came out and sloshed dirty water into the street
and give Wes a swift glance. But he ducked back
inside before Wes could speak to him.

Wes grinned wryly. He walked past the saloon
and, looking across the street, saw that Dave
Bettes was back inside his office. He broke his

153

stride, then thought better of it. He'd have his talk with Bettes after he had seen Ball Hotchkiss—

Behind him, the saloon batwings creaked audibly. Then he heard Vic Arness' voice. "Hold it up, fella! I'm puttin' you under arrest!"

Wes turned slowly, sensing a nervous undercurrent in the deputy's taut voice.

Vic was standing on the walk in front of the saloon. He was facing the Army scout with a Colt cocked and leveled in his hand. His face was paler than usual.

"What for?" Wes asked coldly.

"For breaking out of jail, manhandling a representative of the law, and for suspected stage robbery!" Vic's voice was deliberately loud.

Martin studied the man. There was more than the stated intention of arresting him behind Vic's stand. There was murder in the deputy's eyes. The man was waiting only for the slimmest excuse to gun him down. Out of the corners of his eye Wes saw Dave Bettes come to the doorway of his office, and now he knew why Vic Arness had braced him this way.

Wes raised his hands shoulder high and forced

a pleasant grin to his lips. "You're the law," he said meekly, and started to walk toward Vic.

The deputy's face mirrored a momentary confusion. This was not going the way he had expected. He took a quick step backward.

"Oh, no, you don't!" he grated. "You stand put, fella! Now lift your gun out of its holster and drop it on the walk!"

Alertness surged through Wes, narrowing his gaze. He saw through Vic's game now; he was too old a hand at this grim business not to have run into the Tucson trick before. Once he dropped his hand to his gun to comply, he was a dead man. Vic Arness could claim, and have witnesses, that he had resisted arrest.

"Drop them!" Vic ordered.

"Go to blazes!" Wes said flatly, and turned his back on the deputy. He took the long chance that it would confuse the killer—that Vic wouldn't dare shoot him in the back in plain sight of the town's watching citizens. But he knew, too, that he would have to beat this man. For Vic was out to kill him, and if it wasn't one way it would be another.

He took a long stride away from the deputy,

155

the skin between his shoulder blades puckering, and caught the sound of Vic's inhaled breath. Wes whirled around then, his right hand blurring, exploding, gouting out into flame and smoke.

Vic's Colt was leveled and cocked—and yet he never fired a shot! He staggered under the tearing impact of Wes' bullet. His right hand jerked upward, and the Colt he was holding slipped out. It landed on the walk beside him and went off, and the bullet gouged wood from the saloon wall.

Vic staggered around, fell against the batwings and sprawled forward on his face inside the saloon. Over him the doors swung back and forth slowly, as if in a creaky requiem.

Wes stood on the walk, a tall, cold-eyed man with a gun in his fist. He put his hard glance on Dave Bettes, and the man stepped back inside the office and closed his door.

Slowly Wes ejected the two spent shells in his Colt and replaced them; he kept looking at the justice of the peace sign over Dave's door, knowing that it was nothing but a mockery.

He'd let Dave squirm awhile yet, he decided, and turned away from the saloon and the man he had just shot.

156

Ah Ling's place held a half-dozen customers who had come crowding to the door at the sound of gunfire. They edged back inside as Wes came up and squirmed nervously in their seats as the Army scout entered. One by one they ate a quick breakfast and left.

Ling's moon face was agitated. He served Wes with unaccustomed speed, retiring to the beaded kitchen doorway to stare like some frightened barn owl at Wes.

Wes finished a leisurely breakfast, built himself a cigaret and smoked part of it over his last cup of coffee. Then he paid for his breakfast and walked out. He walked back to the saloon and noticed that Vic's body had been removed. Probably inside, he thought, and crossed the street to the justice of the peace's office.

There was no one inside, but the door was not locked. Wes walked in and sat down at the desk and propped his feet up on the boot-scarred top. He saw cheroots in the tin box and, appropriating one, lighted up.

Dave Bettes walked in a few minutes later.

Wes said, "Come inside and sit down, Dave."

The evil-smelling man remained in the door-

157

way, studying Wes. Finally he rasped: "You got your nerve, fella. Or maybe it's because you've got so darned few brains!"

"I've got both," Wes said without undue arrogance. He took his feet off the desk. "Close that door and sit down! I want to have a private talk with you."

Dave hesitated. Then he closed the door and came over and stood by the chair Wes had indicated. A grudging admiration shone in his eyes. "Outguns my deputy, then walks in here and helps himself to my cigars. Maybe I'd better listen to you."

Wes grinned. "You've been after me to tell you why I came to Bitter Wells. Well, I'm going to tell you." He put his right palm down on the desk top with a hard slap. "One hundred and fifty thousand dollars, Dave! That's what brought me to Bitter Wells!"

Bettes came around the chair. A narrow distrust showed in his eyes. He sank down slowly on the hard seat. "You're lying," he muttered. "There ain't that much money in the county."

"Think so? Listen," Wes said. "Five men held

158

up the Midnight Limited over in New Mexico five years ago. They got away with one hundred and fifty thousand dollars—Wells Fargo money. Two of them died before they got across the Soapstone badlands. The other three made it to Bitter Wells. They had buried the money in the badlands and made an agreement to meet here in town five years later, when, they hoped, the robbery would be pretty well forgotten. Each man had a map—each man's map was essential to the finding of that buried money again."

Dave licked his lips, like a hyena approaching a carcass. His eyes were cold now, and as wary as an old coyote's with one foot caught in a trap. "And you—?"

"I said three of them got away!" Wes growled. "Oley Jones, Cory Bates and Joe Seltzer!"

He waited, studying Dave's face—and he felt disappointment touch him and turn him cold. Dave's eyes flared with a sudden greed; nothing more.

"Bates is dead!" Dave remembered. "You say you're Joe Seltzer. Then where's this Oley Jones hombre?"

159

Wes shook his head. He had played a long shot and had lost, and now he knew that he would have this man and his bunch of cutthroats to contend with.

"I thought you might tell me," he said. "Oley was supposed to be here yesterday. But you say no strangers except Cory and myself showed up?"

"That's right. There ain't been even a stray dog come to Bitter Wells to stay since Ball Hotchkiss and Dan Rourke arrived four years ago. There's the Steeles, too. But they run a horse ranch—" He broke off, an ugly suspicion crowding into his eyes.

"Cory's dead!" Wes said flatly. "Someone killed him and took the map he was carrying on him. And the man who slugged me last night took mine. Unless—" he scowled at Dave—"you or Vic were lying about it."

"We didn't take anything from you!" Dave said harshly. "We didnt know you were carrying a map, or what it would have been for, anyhow."

Wes pushed back in his chair. "Then Oley Jones has it," he decided. "Help me find Jones, and I'll cut you in for a third of the money."

160

Bettes leaned forward, a thin sneer on his lips. He had figured this tall hombre to be a range detective, but now he saw that he was wrong. The man was someone he could understand, and deal with.

"Maybe you're Joe Seltzer and maybe you're not," he muttered. "But I still run this town. If you want my help you'll cut me in for half—or you'll have more trouble than you ever bargained for!"

Wes made a pretense of considering this offer. Then he nodded. "What are you going to tell the sheriff?"

"Who?"

"The sheriff. You said he'd be riding into Bitter Wells this morning."

"Hah!" Bettes teeth showed like yellowed fangs in a humorless grin. "Sheriff Ventley ain't due in Bitter Wells. Made up that story last night to scare you. Figured you had something important to bring you to this flea-bag town looking for Bates and Jones. We thought you'd talk if we pushed you hard enough."

Wes got to his feet. "Reckon it was your idea, too, to sic Vic on me?"

Bettes shrugged. "Vic didn't need much pushing, fella. He was an arrogant man, Vic was— and he considered himself a fast hand with a gun. Almost as good as Ut—"

He caught himself in time and grinned widely, expansively. "Vic just wasn't good enough, was he?"

"Reckon he wasn't," Wes answered shortly. He walked to the door, where he looked back. "Fifty-fifty," he repeated. At Dave's nod, he added grimly, "Just don't try any tricks. I hate to be crossed."

Bettes walked to the door after him. He waited until Wes was well down the street.

"One hundred and fifty thousand dollars," he muttered. "You're a darn fool if you think I'll settle for less than all of it, fella!"

162

— XI —

— BETTES CALLS HIS HAND —

MIRIAM STEELE shook her head at her father's warning. "I won't get into trouble, Dad," she said firmly. "But I've got to know what happened. Jeff didn't come home last night. And Fantasy showed up early this morning, with someone else's saddle on her—"

"Are you sure it's Jeff you're concerned about?' Brandon asked quietly.

A startled epression came into her eyes at his question. She tried to answer honestly, but she was aware of the core of excitement in herself as she thought of the tall man who had escorted her home last night.

163

"I think Wes can take care of himself," she said. "But I am worried about him, too." She colored slightly. "He could have ridden away— he didn't have to stay here. But he went back to find Jeff—"

Brandon put a hand on his daughter's arm. "I know," he said gently. He looked off, toward town. "It's been hard for you, living here, miles from anywhere—"

"Dad—"

He shushed her. "It isn't right, Miriam. You should have a chance to meet some fine young men—" He paused and smiled understandingly. "He's a bit older than you are—"

"Does it matter?"

"Not if he's a good man." Brandon's eyes were troubled. "I didn't see enough of him to know."

"I trust my heart," Miriam said softly. "He is a good man."

"I hope so," Brandon said.

Mary Steele came to the door behind them. She looked tired and worn; she had not slept well. She looked suspiciously at her husband.

"Where are you going?"

"To look for Jeff," Brandon replied. He shook his head at Miriam's look. "I shouldn't let you go. It's my place—"

"You can't leave me here alone!" Mary said bitterly. She looked at Miriam. "Miriam can go. She rides like a man." Her bitterness hurt Miriam, and she turned away from her father.

"I'll get Mr. Hotchkiss to help," she said quickly. "And I understand the sheriff is due in town today. I won't get into any trouble—"

She started toward the corral where Fantasy, her roan mare, whickered loudly and rubbed her neck against the corral bars.

Brandon stood at the foot of the steps, a man caught between his wife and his daughter. Mary had turned sour, but she was still his wife, and he remembered her when things had been easier. She needed him now more than ever. Miriam did not. Miriam was a woman grown—she needed someone else now.

He waited as Miriam saddled the roan and rode back by the house.

"I'll be back before it gets dark," she said. She looked at her mother for some sign of warmth, but Mary Steele's face was pinched with

165

worry for her son.

"Find Jeff," she said harshly. "You just find Jeff and bring him back home, you hear!"

Miriam nodded.

"Take care of yourself," Brandon said softly as she turned away. He waited until she was far down the road before he turned and limped back to join his wife.

They stood together, looking off, wordless and apart, as though a thousand miles separated them. Finally Brandon said, trying to wipe away the miles, "It's a fine day, Mary. The wind's stopped blowing."

She didn't look at him. "Dust and heat and loneliness," she said bitterly. "I'll die if you keep me here."

"I'm not keeping you here," he said, and now his voice was bitter.

She looked at him. "Aren't you?"

"It was you and Jeff who wanted to come here," he reminded her.

"We couldn't stay in Sandersville. Not after—"

"We didn't have to come here," he interrupted her. He looked off toward the distant desert hills.

In the clear morning air they stood out sharply, desolate and rock-strewn and yet strangely fascinating. He took a deep breath.

"But I'm glad we came."

"You and your daughter!" Mary said harshly.

"She's your daughter, too!" Brandon said. His voice held the sharpness of rebuke.

Mary started to turn away, to go back into the house, but he stopped her. "Mary—don't drive her away."

His wife looked at him, her face pinched and closed. "What do you mean?"

"I mean Miriam's ready to go with the first man who says a few kind words to her." He shook his head. "It's time she married. But don't drive her off."

Mary studied him. "My fault. Everything's my fault. Jeff—"

"No—"

Her voice rose above his. "I'm driving my own daughter away. I've turned Jeff against you. That's what you're saying, isn't it?"

"I'm saying the money has blinded you!" he said harshly. "Money that doesn't belong to us." He was goaded beyond control now. "Yes, Mary

167

—it is your fault! You are driving Miriam away. And you're making your son a thief!"

She stood frozen, staring at him, hating him. Then she turned and went into the house and slammed the door behind her.

Brandon remained on the porch.

He had tried to reach his wife, but he had failed. The door between them was a barrier he couldn't scale. He turned and limped down the steps and started toward the corral. He had his chores to do. . . .

MIRIAM STEELE topped the long ridge midway to town and started down into the glaring wash that snaked along the base of the slope. The day was turning hot again, and the morning clearness was giving way to the heat haze, blurring the distant hills.

There was a quickening in her as she passed the spot where her buggy had overturned and remembered the tall man who had given her a hand.

I acted like a fool, she thought. *I can't expect him to come back.*

Fantasy's sudden snort of alarm interrupted

168

her reverie. The roan mare jerked at his reins and minced off toward the side of the road.

Two men rode out of the brush, onto the road in front of her. They jogged up, flanking her with cold hostility, hemming her in so that she could not make a run for it.

The man on her left, a lean, pock-faced person, reached out and took the reins from her.

He looked at his companion. "Never figgered Big Mack was the kind to give a woman a present, did you, Monte? Especially a cayuse like this."

Utah's voice held a dry humor, but Monte was a humorless man. "Big Mack never gave anything to nobody," he said nasally, "except a beating."

Miriam tried to retrieve her reins from Utah. "Let go of those! This horse belongs to me, not to Big Mack!"

"Is that so?" Utah grinned. "What's yore brand, Miss Steele?"

Miriam said angrily: "She isn't branded. But Fantasy is my horse!"

"Tell you what," Utah murmured. "Let's go on into town and talk to Big Mack—"

She tried to break away, but Utah kept a tight

grip on the reins. "Now that isn't nice," he said. He looked at Monte. "Last time we saw this little mare, Big Mack was riding her, wasn't he?"

Monte nodded. "Called her Queenie."

Frightened now, Miriam beat at Utah's arm, trying to regain her reins. Monte lifted his hand and cuffed her alongside her head.

Miriam gasped, tears of pain glistening in her eyes. "You—you ruffian—"

Utah grinned. "Now, Monte, the lady's right. No gentleman ever hits a lady."

He released his hold on Miriam's reins and slapped her across the mouth.

"Now," he said grimly, "let's not have any more talk from you! Let's just ride on nice and quiet into town and see Big Mack about this mare!"

BALL HOTCHKISS looked up as Wes came into the barn. He was seated on a wooden box in the harness enclosure, mending a bridle. The bridle slipped from his fingers and he cursed harshly, his nerves raw, apprehension flickering in his eyes.

"You're asking for trouble, mister. And I don't

170

want to be a part of it—"

"You don't have to be," Wes cut in coldly. "Just tell me where Jeff is hiding out.'

Ball licked his lips. "I haven't seen the kid since he—"

"Since last night!" Wes said sharply. He stood over Ball, tall and immovable and impatient. "You rode out to see him right after I left here with Miss Steele." He motioned to the mule peering at them over the bars of his stall. "You told me you were the only man Sampson let ride him. He was still warm when I checked in last night."

Ball slowly laid the harness aside. "All right," he muttered. "I did see Jeff last night. Brought him some supplies—"

He stood up. "I've known the Steele family since they came here. Jeff's like my own son. After his run-in with Big Mack, he decided to hide out for a spell—"

"He should have gone home!"

Ball shrugged. "I'm not his father." At Wes' look, he grinned wryly. "I said he's like my son, far as I'm concerned. But Jeff's a pretty stubborn kid—"

171

"Jeff's not hiding out because of Big Mack, and you know it!" Wes interrupted. He's after that money, any way he can get hold of it! And you're helping him!"

"Me?" Ball made a gesture of innocence. "Look, Joe—I mean Mister Martin—I don't need money. And I always thought it was just a pipe dream about those holdup men catching a hundred and fifty thousand dollars out in the badlands somewhere—"

"It's no pipe dream!"

Ball shrugged. "If you say so."

"I don't care who gets the money," Wes said. "But the boy's in danger. I promised his father I'd bring the boy home."

"He won't come easy," Ball warned.

"Don't expect him to," Wes answered. He studied Ball. "You know the kid was in Bates' room at the Mesa House last night, don't you?"

Ball's eyes widened in surprise. "No, I don't."

"I didn't want to tell his sister—she has enough troubles. But he was there, waiting, when I walked in. He was the one who slugged me, took the map Joe Seltzer had given me—"

Ball shook his head. "I don't believe it."

"You don't have to!" Wes snapped. "Just show me where he's hiding before Oley Jones figgers it out and gets to him first!"

"Jones? But you said last night Jones didn't show up."

"He didn't show up yesterday," Wes agreed, "because Jones was already in Bitter Wells. Had been for years, waiting. Changed his name and his identity, and waited for the years to go by. Waited for Cory Bates and Joe Seltzer to show up, so he could kill them both. Because he never intended to split that money three ways."

Ball shifted nervously. "Who is Jones?" He glanced toward the open door, and fear tightened his face. "Dave Bettes?"

"Maybe. I'm not sure." Wes frowned. "But it can't be anybody else. That's why I tried to bring him out into the open by telling him when I had come to town. I let him think I was Joe Seltzer. If he's Oley Jones, then he knows I'm lying. And if I'm right about him, then he's worrying right now about who I really am."

Ball wiped his brow with his neckerchief. "If he is this Oley Jones, he'll never let you get out of this town alive, Wes. And if he knows Jeff

173

has that map—"

"We have to get to Jeff first!" Wes said grimly.

Ball nodded.

"It just occurred to me," Wes added, "that if Bettes isn't Oley Jones, then the real Oley Jones is in a sweat right now. Because Dave Bettes isn't the kind to let a hundred and fifty thousand dollars slip through his fingers!"

Ball turned toward the stalls. "I'll take you to Jeff myself," he said. Faint beads of sweat glistened on his face. "But we better not leave town together, not after what you just told me about Dave." He turned to the door and pointed to the southwest. "I'll ride out first. Meet me by that small butte in about an hour."

Wes fixed the landmark in his mind. "In an hour," he agreed.

He saddled his big roan horse and rode down the ramp and out onto Bitter Wells' main street. The wind was starting to blow again—not hard, but insistently. He wondered if it was blowing sand over one hundred and fifty thousand dollars.

He turned the animal toward the hotel and

174

dismounted and walked inside the Mesa House. He wanted to ask Kenny, the desk clerk, something that had been nagging at him for a long time. . . .

Kenny wasn't in. The old man who was taking his place said he didn't know when Kenny would be back. The boy had spells sometimes, the old man added. "Holes up in his room at home and won't see anybody for mebbe a day or two. . . ."

Wes came out to the hotel veranda and stood undecided. He had time to kill before joining Hotchkiss, but he didn't want to set himself up as a target for Dave Bettes.

The danger came unexpectedly from another quarter!

Riders came up from the south, jogging into town. Three of them. But it was the rider in the middle who held Wes motionless, sent a sliver of fear through him.

The rider was Miriam Steele. She looked dazed, and there was a cut on her lip marked by flecks of dried blood.

Wes stepped down from the veranda, intercepting them. The two men flanking the girl reined in abruptly at the sight of him.

175

Wes said tightly: "Miriam—keep riding!"

Miriam's eyes lifted to him; a spark of feeling flared in them.

"Wes," she whispered.

Monte put a hand in front of her, holding her back. "Whoa!" he said coldly. "You're not going anywhere." He looked at Utah. "Who is he?"

Utah shook his head.

Wes' body was rigid. He couldn't make a play while Miriam remained between them.

"Let her go!" he said.

Utah grinned wolfishly. "Not until we see Big Mack. She stole his horse—"

"Big Mack's a liar!" Wes said bleakly.

Utah went rigid. His eyes narrowed on Wes, then flicked to Monte, and he nodded slowly.

Monte said: "Yore name Joe Seltzer?"

Wes knew what was coming. He said: "Miriam —ride!" and went for his Colt as Utah drew, not waiting for his answer. He shaded the pock-faced killer by a hair, his bullet lifting Utah out of the saddle, dropping him into the dust beneath Fantasy's mincing feet.

He outdrew Utah, but Monte would have gotten him. The outlaw had his gun out and muzzle tilting downward when Miriam rode her mare directly into the muzle blast.

The bullet tore through the mare's neck, and the animal reared wildly, dying, and fell backward, sending Miriam tumbling out of the saddle.

Wes killed Monte before the killer had a chance for another shot!

Miriam lay momentarily stunned. Wes started for her, a clawing fear in him. "Miriam," he said hoarsely, and only then realized how much the girl meant to him.

He knelt beside her. She stirred and turned toward him, and her eyes suddenly dilated at something in back of him.

"Wes!" Her voice caught in her throat. "Behind you! Dave Bet—"

Wes whirled up and around as the rifle bullet went by him. He saw Dave turn and run, and he held his fire. Instead, he took off after the man, who ducked into the alley between his office and the building next to it.

Gun in hand, Wes followed.

The phony justice of the peace made a ludicrous figure in his Prince Albert coat, tails flapping wildly, as he ran. He reached the far end of the alley and brought up against a sagging board fence. He wasn't spry enough to hurdle it. He turned swiftly, reacting like a cornered rat.

He fired at Wes, levering two wild shots before Wes' return fire smashed him back against the board fence. He slid down and tried to crawl away.

Wes came to stand over him. He had not wanted to kill this man, but Bettes had given him no choice.

Dave stared up at him with eyes already glazing. "Didn't mean to cross you, Joe . . . just didn't have time to tell Utah and Monte not to kill. . . ."

The breath went out of him then, and he sagged down into the alley dirt.

Wes stood over him a moment, then knelt down and searched the man. But if Bettes was Oley Jones, he didn't have his map, or Cory Bates', on him.

Wes left him there and ran back to the street. A small group had collected around Miriam, who was on her feet, dazed, shaken, but not badly hurt.

Wes pushed through to her. She reacted with a small cry of relief and went into his arms, crying softly. He held her close for a moment, then looked at a matronly woman standing nearby.

"Is there a doctor in town?"

The woman shook her head.

Wes gently pushed Miriam toward her. "Take care of her."

Miriam clung to him. "No. I'm all right. Stay with me, Wes!"

He said, "I'll be back, Miriam."

He pushed her into the matronly woman's arms. "I'll be back—with Jeff."

He ran to his horse and mounted. Miriam watched him ride off. Then her eyes went to Fantasy, lying still in the road.

She sagged against the woman, her eyes closing.

"That's all right," the woman said, holding her. "He'll be back. . . ."

She fixed a couple of men with a stern glance. "Here, Jake, Simp—give me a hand with her. Can't leave her out in the sun like this!"

Her gaze swept to the others. "The rest of

you clean up this mess. And somebody better ride to Caldwell for the sheriff!"

She followed behind Jake and Simp as they carried Miriam to her house.

— XII —

— THE MAN CALLED OLEY JONES —

BALL HOTCHKISS was waiting for Wes in
the lee of the small butte when the Army scout
rode up. A tumbleweed blew across his path,
rolling toward its nameless destiny. The flats
were shrouded in blowing sand.

Ball was mounted on Sampson. Wes noticed
that his saddlebags bulged, and the thought occurred to Wes that the man had come prepared
for a long journey. The stableman was carrying
a rifle in his saddle boot, and he was wearing an
old holster and gunbelt around his hips, cinched
under his paunch. The walnut-handled Colt
Miriam had lowered to Wes in Dave's back room
jail jutted from his belt.

Ball caught Wes' probing glance and said glibly: "Dave Bettes might have smelled out something, Wes. I thought I'd pack this gun along, just in case we ran into trouble."

"Bettes is dead," Wes said. "So are two of his men, Utah and Monte."

Hotchkiss twisted in his saddle to look at him, surprise on his face. "Dead?"

Wes nodded grimly. "Ran into them just before I left town."

He was thinking of Dave Bettes' dying statement, and it occurred to him that things seldom went the way men planned them. Dave had sent for Utah and Monte to kill Wes before he had his talk with him, and then had changed his mind, too late. . . .

Hotchkiss neck-reined his mule to a stop. His face seemed strained. "Did you find out if Dave was this Oley Jones you're looking for?"

Wes shook his head. "Dave died without saying." He made a wry gesture. "Reckon we'll never find the money now, but I guess that doesn't matter so much, as long as we find the kid."

Ball licked his lips. "Somebody has those

maps you told me about—"

"Jeff has one—the one he took from me," Wes said. He tapped his coat pocket. "I have Cory Bates'—"

"Cory's? I thought you said Oley Jones killed him and took his map."

"Oley killed Bates. But he didn't find a map on him." Wes smiled faintly at the look in Ball's eyes. "Because Cory didn't trust either of his two companions. Just in case he was double-crossed, he mailed his map to himself in Bitter Wells." He paused. "Pop Willis had the latter, and was looking for Bates, when I took it from him." He shook his head. "But it takes all three maps to find the Wells Fargo money, Ball. And Oley Jones, wherever he is, has the other one."

Ball licked his lips. "You think he's dead?"

"Could be," Wes answered. "He didn't show up in town after all."

Ball muttered: "Jeff'll be mighty disappointed. Since I knew him, he's been counting on that money."

"He'll get over it," Wes answered shortly.

They rode west, making a strange pair—a tall, wide-shouldered man in Army scout garb and a

183

short, paunchy man mounted on a mule. They rode along the edge of the lava beds, and finally Ball turned into the narrow fissure leading toward ugly black hills which ages past had spewed forth a black and forbidding mass of jagged rocks.

Ball grew quieter as they rode deeper into the lava bed. He seemed to scrunch down in his saddle, become small and thoughtful.

About a mile inside the lava crack, Ball suddenly reined aside.

"The kid's real jumpy," he said tensely. "Would be better if I rode on ahead and set him straight about you first—"

"We'll ride in on him together," Wes said coldly. "I'll take my chances with Jeff."

Ball shrugged.

They rounded an overhang of black rock and came into a small clearing. Ahead of them was the rising slant of a boulder-strewn hill, bare and ugly in the waning afternoon sun.

The remains of a campfire were visible in the clearing. Ball rode up to the embers and dismounted. He glanced down at the charred remains of the fire and glanced up at Wes.

"Looks like he's cleared out," he muttered. He stepped away from his mule, then pivoted quickly, spry for his age.

"All right, Jeff!" he cried out. . . .

Wes was pivoting toward Hotchkiss when the heavy report of a Colt from the rocks to his right caught him by surprise. The bullet hit him high up in his right shoulder and knocked him out of the saddle.

He fell heavily and rolled away from the mule, who was lashing out wildly with both hind legs. He caught a glimpse of Hotchkiss with his gun in his hand, trying to cut down on him.

He rolled away from the first shot, clenching his teeth against the pain. He slipped his Colt free and fired once as he rolled again, and it was a lucky shot. It smashed Ball's forearm, sending his Colt spinning from him.

Ball sank to his knees, clutching his arm, blood spurting through his fingers. Pain glazed his eyes.

"Jeff!" he yelled. "Kill him!"

Wes lurched to his feet and swung around to face the boy who came out of the rocks. Jeff stopped, eyeing the gun in Wes' hand. His des-

185

perate gaze went to Hotchkiss.

"Kill him!" Ball screamed.

Jeff hesitated. Wes said: "Throw that gun down, kid!"

Ball lunged to his feet. "Blast you, Jeff—you want that money; kill him! He's got Cory Bates' map—"

Jeff brought his gun up. Wes fired, and Jeff flinched and dropped his gun, staring at the back of his hand where Wes' bullet had gouged.

Ball lunged for his Colt. He scooped it up and swung around to Wes, and Wes shot twice, deliberately. Ball fell over backward and didn't move.

Wes stood on braced feet, fighting the blackness that threatened to engulf him. He made a gesture to Jeff with his Colt.

"Come here!" he said thinly.

The boy held back just long enough to show defiance, then obeyed.

"Search him!" Wes said. "You'll find a map on him."

Jeff stared at him.

Wes reached into his pocket and took out the envelope containing Cory Bates' section of the map. He tossed it at Jeff's feet.

"There's Bates' part of the map," he said tonelessly. "With the one you took from me last night, you've got them all." He motioned with his Colt. "Go ahead—search Jones!"

"Jones?" Jeff looked down at Hotchkiss' body.

Wes nodded. "Oley Jones."

Jeff said tightly, "He was my father's friend!"

"Jones was nobody's friend," Wes said. "He waited in Bitter Wells for Bates and Joe Seltzer to show up. But he wanted that money all for himself."

Jeff knelt beside the dead man, searching him. He found the map in the man's wallet. He looked up at Wes, his face pale.

Wes swayed slightly on his feet. "Five men died for that money," he said grimly. "Your father spent three years in a prison cell. But it's all yours now, kid."

Jeff's jaws tightened. He took a step backward, toward the rocks.

Wes said: "You'll put your father back in prison. And you'll be on the run for the rest of your life. But maybe it's worth it. One hundred and fifty thousand dollars is a lot of money."

187

Jeff said bitterly: "It belongs to us, mister. Dad paid for it—and Mother!"

He stopped, looking at Wes. "You're not going to let me go," he said harshly. "You want the money for yourself. You'll shoot me in the back—"

Wes tossed his gun at Jeff's feet.

"It's your choice, kid," he said. "You've got to make it yourself."

He turned and started for his horse, ground-reined a few yards away. But his legs buckled under him before he reached the animal, and he fell face down in the gritty sand.

Jeff eyed the unconscious man for a long while. Then he picked up the Colt Wes had thrown at his feet and walked back to him.

Wes stirred as Jeff tried to hoist him across the roan's saddle. He was too heavy for Jeff to manage. He pushed the boy aside and clung to the saddle, his gaze clearing.

"I'll manage," he said. "You have a horse?"

Jeff nodded. "In the rocks—back there."

He came back a few moments later, riding a bay mare. Sampson pulled away from him as he tried to reach out and take the mule's bridle.

188

"Let him be," Wes said. "He'll find his way home."

"What about—him?" Jeff motioned to Hotchkiss, alias Oley Jones.

Wes shrugged. "Guess we should take him back, what's left of him." He took a deep breath. "You'll have to do it alone. I can't help."

He watched Jeff tote the dead man up across his saddle, then mount up. Jeff glanced back into the badlands.

"What about the money?"

"It'll keep," Wes grunted. "It's kept for five years. A few days more or less won't matter now."

He swung away from the dead campfire. "Your sister is waiting for you in town. She'll be glad to see you . . ."

WES MARTIN recuperated at the Steele ranch. He had an attentive and attractive nurse in Miriam. And no one mentioned the money still buried somewhere out in the Soapstone badlands; not even Mary Steel, who seemed to suffer his presence in her house because he had brought her son back.

189

It was as though the stolen money had suddenly become taboo in the Steele house.

But when the sheriff came to the ranch to question him, Wes told him about the money. He didn't mention the Steele family's part in the story. But he told the rest of it straight.

The sheriff rode with him and Jeff out into the desert. They found the money, with the help of the three maps Wes handed over to the lawman.

Sheriff Ventley whistled as he riffled through the still crisp money. "Many men would kill for a whole lot less," he said. He looked at Wes. "You could have picked it up and been in Mexico before anyone got wind of it, mister."

Wes looked at Jeff. Jeff's smile was strained. "I could have," Wes said. "But it wouldn't have been worth it."

The sheriff scratched his head. "Guess it wouldn't," he said softly. "But I remember a reward being posted at the time of the holdup. I imagine it still holds good. Pretty good stake for a wandering man."

Wes grinned. "Thanks, Sheriff. But I'm planning on staying. Might even start me a small horse ranch. . . ."

They parted from the sheriff in Bitter Wells. Jeff said: "Sis's waiting, Wes." His tone had a teasing friendliness. "Might take Ma a while to get used to calling you son-in-law, but I'm betting she'll come around!"

"I hope so," Wes said. Then he grinned. "Beat you home, Jeff!"

He put his big stallion into a run for the ranch where Miriam was waiting.

Jeff didn't even try to catch up.

Peter B. Germano was born the oldest of six children in New Bedford, Massachusetts. During the Great Depression, he had to go to work before completing high school. It left him with a powerful drive to continue his formal education later in life, finally earning a Master's degree from Loyola University in Los Angeles in 1970. He sold his first Western story to A.A. Wyn's Ace Publishing magazine group when he was twenty years old. In the same issue of *Sure-Fire Western* (1/39) Germano had two stories, one by Peter Germano and the other by Barry Cord. He came to prefer the Barry Cord name for his Western fiction. When the Second World War came, he joined the U.S. Marine Corps. Following the war he would be called back to active duty, again as a combat correspondent, during the Korean conflict. In 1948 Germano began publishing a series of Western novels, either as Barry Cord or **Jim Kane**, stories notable for their complex plots while the scenes themselves are simply set, with a minimum of description and quick character sketches employed to establish a wide assortment of very different personalities. The pacing, which often seems swift due to the adept use of a parallel plot structure (narrating a story from several different viewpoints), is combined in these novels with atmospheric descriptions of weather and terrain. *Dry Range* (1955), *The Sagebrush Kid* (1954), *The Iron Trail Killers* (1960), and *Trouble in Peaceful Valley* (1968) are among his best Westerns. "The great southwest . . ." Germano wrote in 1982, "this is the country, and these are the people that gripped my imagination . . . and this is what I have been writing about for forty years. And until I die I shall remain the little New England boy who fell in love with the 'West,' and as a man had the opportunity to see it and live in it."